# THE REAL KINGS OF CLEVELAND

## KALITA STOKES

*I would like to dedicate this book to my beautiful and intelligent daughter, Aurrion, and my wonderful son, Wayne. You two are the best things that ever happened to me, and God broke the mold when he made you. Y'all give me life and the strength to continue on when I don't think I can. I love y'all, and I dedicate the success of this book to you.*

# ACKNOWLEDGMENTS

I want to acknowledge my beautiful niece, Camille. You introduced me the world of urban fiction, and I can't thank you enough for that. You had me read a book that was written by Jahquel J, and it changed my life by helping me through one of the toughest times of my life. Thank you, and I love you.

I would also like to acknowledge my siblings; Tonda, Michelle, and Eric. Thanks for making me believe I can do anything I put my mind to and having my back whenever times get hard.

# HOME SWEET HOME

Dr. Samantha Howard-Matthews
**"Sam"**

DR. SAMANTHA HOWARD sounded so good rolling off people's tongue when they called my name. It took me a long time to become a doctor and gain the confidence to be proud of the African-American queen I had transformed into.

When I started college, it was strange being one of the few poor, black girls going to a rich school like Harvard. The first week I arrived in Boston was a rough one for me. I was having a hard time transitioning into my new life and environment. At times, I would become mentally and physically ill and had panic attacks left and right. Plus, my anxiety was through the roof due to fear. I was scared someone would snatch the opportunity to go away to college away from me at any moment.

I constantly walked around with so many emotions running throughout my body, causing sleepless nights, nausea, and even throwing up constantly. I was homesick too, and I know that sounds crazy, but I was. It wasn't that I was missing home, because we both know that's not true, but I was missing the consistency of my everyday life that I was used to, regardless of how bad it was. Even though my normal was abuse, I went through that every day for eighteen years. So it wasn't easy letting that part of my life go and letting my walls down in order to allow others in. It took me eighteen years to build that wall, so it took time for me to trust others enough to allow the wall to come down. It took a little while, but eventually, I established new and healthy norms. I made new friends, and I joined different support groups and clubs. I was living my best life and loving every minute of it.

Maybe two months into my freshman year at Harvard, I met my future husband, Brian Matthews. Initially, we met after we both joined a group established for students that received the Dreams Beyond Measure scholarships. This scholarship was developed by a Harvard alumnus who came from the slums of Detroit, and when she started school there in the eighties, the more privileged students made her feel like she didn't belong. They made her feel like she wasn't good or smart enough to be there. She had no support from the administration, and when she felt she couldn't take the pressure of being the outcast anymore and contemplated dropping out, she met her future husband. He came from old money, so ten years ago, they started a Harvard-based scholarship, and that's how many of us were able to afford to attend the prestigious school.

The group provided members with counseling, vouchers for clothing, meals, and an array of other things. The group is how I met my husband, Brian Matthews. We were classmates, and he would flirt with me every time he saw me, but I would never agree to go out with him. It took a year for him to break me down before I agreed to go on a date with him. We started out as friends, and that's why things moved so quickly between us. We got married, graduated college, and I had Kassidy while we were both going through our residencies. Due to life-changing events, we both decided it would be best if we separated and divorced.

When I left for college, I vowed I would never come back to Cleveland, and that's why I was teetering back and forth for months, with my best friend, Camille, threatening to beat my ass, before I mustered up enough courage to apply for the pediatric job at Cleveland Clinic. Ever since I finished my residency years ago, my brother, Bennie, has been trying to get me to come work at Cleveland Clinic with him, but he knew that wasn't an option for me because I never wanted to move back. Honestly, if it wasn't for me getting divorced, I might not have even contemplated returning to my "home sweet home."

Bennie was so extra when I told him that I finally applied for a job at Cleveland Clinic that when the time came for my face-to-face interview with human resources, he paid for a jet to pick me and Kassidy up from Boston Logan International Airport the morning of the interview. He paid for me and Kassidy's suite at the Hilton downtown until Sunday, and I took a first-class flight back.

It didn't take long for human resources to decide which applicant was better suited for the job, because yes, they offered your girl the job a couple of days later. It came with a six-figure salary, medical benefits, and other perks that made the job sweet for me. The best part of it all was I got to work at the same hospital as my big bro. I've asked him plenty of times if he helped me lock down the job, but he says he didn't. Even if he didn't help me get the position, he did help me with the offer human resources offered me being so sweet. Don't get it twisted, I'm very excited my brother is the director of the emergency department, and I can't give two fucks if his influence helped sweeten the deal for me. I hate when people be like, *I want to get the job on my own!* Fuck that! As said in the movie, *The Player's Club,* "Gotta use what you got, to get what you want." I couldn't say it better if I wanted to.

It was my last day of the two-month training course I had to complete and pass in the emergency room. All doctors were required to pass the training before they were allowed to start a position on any inpatient floor taking care of patients. Our preceptor already informed us all that we passed, so this last day was just a formality. The emergency room manager and our preceptor decided to throw us a goodbye potluck to celebrate our last day. I guess they only did this for the exceptional physicians, like myself. Just playing, just playing! But Bennie said they threw potlucks for the physicians that became assets to the emergency team during their training.

Bennie also let me know why the training was a requirement now. See, my group was the first group required to take this training because Bennie originally developed it for new residents and new doctors. With all the complaints of malpractice and lawsuits, the board decided it wouldn't hurt to have all new hires have some extra training. Human resources even went as far as to make the training a requirement now, and the staff in the emergency room said we did a really good job, and we went above and beyond for our patients. It also didn't hurt that we were all good looking.

Ummm, how would I describe myself? I'm an African-American bombshell, six feet tall with a slim-thick frame, size 36DD breasts due to breast reconstruction, a nice, apple-bottom ass, caramel complexion, big, hazel eyes with a light-green rim that my mother passed on to me, and may I add I've never seen anyone with the exact same sclera as me? I have full eyebrows that look tattooed on, long, natural, black eyelashes and natural, jet-black hair that hangs down to the middle of my back when straightened. Eating healthy had become part of my life ever since I was diagnosed with breast cancer diagnosis almost five years ago. My abs are well defined, and I worked out three days a week and maintained a healthy diet to keep them that way.

This morning, when I picked out my clothes, I decided to dress it up a little since it was the last day, and I knew we weren't going to be doing much so I wanted to be cute. Let's just say I can be a label whore at times, and I'm not ashamed to admit it, but it made it hard narrowing down a decision because I did have a small shopping addiction, so I had a lot of options. I decided on an all-black, lace Gucci dress that has black, sheer lace across the abdomen and stopped right above my knees. After much indecisiveness, I chose to wear my all-black red bottoms with gold spikes coming out of them with a peep toe. My toenails had a freshly-painted white French-manicure tip. I beat my face to the gods, and I flat-ironed my jet-black hair straight, causing it to hang down to the middle of my back. I wore my white lab coat that I had *Dr. Samantha Howard* stitched across the right breast area, and I was feeling myself.

As I sat behind the nurse's station daydreaming, one of the nurses slapped my shoulder, warning me that my preceptor was headed our way. Truly, I didn't give a fuck, but because it was my brother's department, I wanted to leave on a good note. I stood and picked up the iPad for the last time to treat my last patient in the emergency room. After that, I would be off for two weeks, and then I would start my position in the main part of the hospital.

As I pulled up the list in the queue, I clicked on and accepted the first patient I saw. I opened up his medical record and noticed the reason the patient had come in to be treated and saw the symptoms he'd been experiencing. The patient's name was Kingston James Jr. He was an eight-year-old African-American male that had been experiencing stomach pain for the last four days. As I scanned past his name, it seemed familiar, but I couldn't figure out why. I let it go, because eventually, it would come to me. His vital signs showed he had a temperature, low blood pressure, and a rapid heartbeat. While I stood outside of the room, I sanitized my hands with the sanitizer next to the door's entrance, and then I proceeded to walk into the room and introduce myself. As I walked inside, I saw a dark-skinned woman sitting next to the bed that the child was lying in, so I assumed the woman was his mother.

"Hello. My name is Dr. Samantha Matthews, and I've been assigned to treat this little guy here, "I said as I put my right hand out to shake the woman's hand, and she did the same.

"I'm Tammy, KJ's mother," she spoke nervously, and her voice started cracking like she was attempting to hold back tears. Or she might have just been nervous because she smelled like someone poured a bottle of tequila over her whole body right before she walked in the ER. I'm just saying!

I asked her, "What caused you to bring your son in today?"

"Well, for the last three days, KJ has been saying his stomach pains, and last night, the pain was really bad, so I decided to bring him in today after we woke up." She turned to him and rubbed and kissed his forehead in a lovingly manner.

"Hey, big guy, can you tell me your name, and if you can remember your birthday?" He nodded his head up and down, then recited it for me.

"Is it okay if I listen to your heart and stomach with this funny-looking thing?" When he looked my way, I began dangling one end of the stethoscope while the other end laid clipped around my neck. Again, he nodded his head up and down slowly. "And is it okay for me to touch your belly? I'm going to do my very best not to hurt you, OK?" I softly asked, and again, without speaking, he nodded his head up and down but was slower this time.

"It's OK, ma'am, for you to take care of me, and can you call me KJ, please?" Kingston Jr. said.

I was really taken aback by how mild mannered and respectful the little boy was. As I listened to his heart, it sounded strong, and the noises his stomach was making were normal. The problem was when I went to touch his stomach, it caused him an enormous amount of pain, and immediately, I knew it was his appendix due to the location of the pain. I put in orders for him to receive IV fluids, pain medication, and for his blood to be drawn for laboratory tests. I also ordered for a CAT scan to be done. The scans would provide the images I needed to see what was going on inside his stomach. Once all the orders were placed, I focused on placing the surgical consult in the computer. With the referral placed, I decided to light a fire under surgery's ass, because if not, it would have been an hour before someone came down to do an assessment on KJ. I called the operating-room coordinator and asked her to send a surgeon down to do an assessment and see if my patient needed surgery. She put me on hold to go check and see which surgeon was available to come down to the emergency room.

As I sat at the nurse's station on hold, waiting on the surgery coordinator to pick the phone back up, I noticed a nurse going into KJ's room, and I assumed it was to start the orders I had already put into the system. I was glad because I was going to find her next, or I was just going to complete the orders myself. I'm not one of those people whose job stops at my title, and I can't stand a worker who feels that way. Especially in healthcare! There are plenty of times I stepped in and did the job of EVS, dietary, nursing assistant, nurse, and doctor, and I've even provided a patient with surgical services before. As long as the patient is safe, and it's within my scope of practice, I'll do it or make sure it gets done. I wish people would stop being so lazy, because the next person that tells one of my patients, "that's not my job," my petty ass was going to make it my mission as long as I worked there to get their sorry asses fired. Real talk!

Once the coordinator informed me the surgeons would be down shortly, I headed over to KJ's room to update his mom on how things were progressing, and I also wanted to let her know what I thought was going on. I knocked on the door and sanitized my hands before entering the room. "Mrs. James, I ordered for a CAT scan to be performed on KJ because I have a feeling the problem is his appendix, and if I'm correct, then KJ will have to have surgery to have it removed. The surgeons will be down immediately after he comes back from getting his CAT scan. This will allow time for the scans to be uploaded into our system, and the doctors will be able to pull the scans up anywhere in the hospital. I'll be here for a couple more hours today, so feel free to have his nurse page me if you have any questions that you need to be answered. It was nice meeting you, Mrs. James, and I'm sorry we had to meet under these circumstances." I reached my hand out to shake hers again, and she accepted my gesture all while thanking me. Then she pulled me into a hug, and the entire time we hugged her entire body was shaking hysterically.

She broke the hug and started crying, and then she began frantically typing on her cell phone. After texting for a few minutes, she outright started calling who I assumed was KJ's father over and over again. Eventually, he answered her call, and she recited everything I had told her since they had been here. When she finally stopped talking, he started yelling through the phone at her so loud she almost dropped it. He scared the hell out of me, so I know she was shaking in her boots. I smoothly exited stage left and didn't stop walking until I reached the break room, where the potluck was actively going on. The staff had sandwiches, chips, fruit trays, and cake to celebrate the end of our training. I socialized for a bit with the doctors and staff, but I couldn't really enjoy myself because I was so worried about KJ.

Approximately an hour later, I grabbed my iPad and headed back toward KJ's room. As I walked in, I noticed a man in his room with his back to the door's entrance. Even though I couldn't see the front of his body, I could tell the man was tall with a nice build, and he had freshly-twisted dreads hanging freely down to the middle of his back. Dreads had been my thing ever since I dated my ex who had dreads damn near our entire relationship.

Just the profile from the back led me to believe he was sexy as fuck. I assumed it was KJ's father, the man she spoke with earlier when I was in the room. I took a few steps into the room while looking down at the iPad because I was looking up the KJ's completed test results, but when I looked up, I almost pissed myself. I came face-to-face with an African-American god, and when he turned around, I was looking at Mr. Muthafuckin' Kingston James himself. *God's really trying me right now*, I thought to myself. What was crazy was, I should have put two and two together when I first saw the name, but it was just so much going on, I didn't really pay attention to it but I didn't, due to me only paying attention to KJ's symptoms that he presented with, so his name went straight over my head.

I immediately dropped the iPad, turned around, and ran out of the room nervously. I heard KJ's mother ask King what the fuck was that about as I ran into the first restroom I could find. Once the door shut, I leaned against the door trying to catch my breath. I closed my eyes and tears just cascaded down my face. I felt like my heart was beating a mile a minute, all while it was trying to jump out of my chest. If I didn't calm myself down, this would turn into a full-blown panic attack, which I couldn't allow to happen.

"I can't believe I just saw King," I whispered to myself. I hadn't seen this man in a quite some time. It was almost six years ago at my brother's birthday party the last time I saw him. Let's just say avoidance is a virtue in my book, so I did everything I could to prevent us from crossing paths before that night. The only reason it happened then is because I was ready to confront that part of my past, and I thought it would help me get over him, but it had the opposite effect, and I had craved the man ever since.

After a few minutes, I began to calm down. I knew I needed to get back in there. I had no choice because I had a patient to treat. I looked in the mirror, grabbed my gloss out of my pocket, and applied a thin coat on my lips while looking over my makeup. Yes, it was still flawless, but my stomach started bubbling from the nerves. The thought had my silly ass laughing at myself, and the laugh is just what the doctor ordered because my stomach settled right on down. I glanced in the mirror once more and exited the restroom, headed straight for KJ's room.

I didn't want to just barge in, so I knocked on the door a couple of times and waited for approval to enter. Once I heard it was OK for me to enter, I pushed the door open and stepped inside, and I couldn't take my eyes off of King, and he definitely couldn't take his eyes off of me.

I was trying my best to keep it professional because I didn't know if he had spoken to KJ's mother about me or what had been said around her. "Hello, Mr. Kingston James. I'm the doctor treating who I assume is your handsome son, KJ," I asked as I held my hand out for him to shake. The look he gave me was like I offended him by calling him Kingston. I don't think in all the years I've known him I have ever called him Kingston.

"Yes, this is my handsome son you notice he takes after his pops in the good looks department," Kingston stated and he wasn't lying with his fine ass. He took a step forward and leaned in towards my ear, and every hair on my body stood at attention in anticipation of his next move. I closed my eyes waiting for his raspy, deep voice to serenade my eardrums. "So it's Kingston now? That's how we're doing it now, *ma*? A nigga can't get a hug or a kiss, because the last time I checked, we didn't do handshakes. Plus, I haven't seen you in quite some time," he teased, and I smiled feeling antsy because I hadn't been in his presence in such a long time.

I leaned in, and gave him a hug and the smell of his cologne made my 'kitty' thump. I needed to get away from him before I pulled him into the bathroom so he could scratch the itch I was feeling. I tried to break free from the hug but he had me in a death grip and he didn't release me until he was ready. I felt like he did that shit on purpose to get under 'ole girl' skin.

"Can you tell me what's going on with him? Dr. Samantha Matthews, correct," King asked, acting like he was trying to figure out her name

"Let me pull up his medical record real quick before I update you on what's going on with KJ," I responded. "So I believe KJ has something called appendicitis, which means his appendix is infected. By KJ's test results and how much pain KJ's in, I believe he needs to have surgery as soon as possible, so the doctors can remove his appendix. He should only have to stay in the hospital a couple of days after surgery, and once he's home he'll have to take it easy for a few more days, but after that he should be good as new." I had to break eye contact because his stare was so intense. I looked down at the iPad while I finished talking, trying my best to get my emotions in check. I couldn't let him see me sweat. *Shit, Sam, get it together,* I thought to myself as I continued the conversation.

"Is surgery really necessary for KJ to get better?" King questioned.

"Yes. If it was caught earlier, his pediatrician could have tried antibiotics first, but now he needs to have it removed. Also, while he's here, his doctor will also order for him to receive a couple of antibiotics to make sure the infection is completely gone," I explained further.

Before I could ask them if they had questions, the surgeons rushed in, and one began assessing KJ while the other spoke with his parents. The surgeons began explaining the surgery they would be performing on KJ to his parents, and once they finished, King signed the consent form. The surgical tech walked in and unlocked KJ's bed and started pushing him out of the room, en route to the operating room. I walked the group to the elevators, and once they began to pile in, I turned to head back to the ER in the opposite direction. I took two

small steps, then quickly turned, and headed back toward the elevators and stuck my hand inside to give King one of my business cards
with my contact information on it. "King, call me if you have questions or just need to talk." Tammy mugged me hard as hell like I had
two fucks to give about her. I headed back to the ER with a smile on
my face thinking about the possibilities.

Mr. Kingston James' fine ass was the total opposite of my ex-
husband, Brian. I really wasn't trying to compare the two, but they
were truly night and day. King stood approximately six feet seven
inches tall, and his light gray-colored eyes that gave him a mysterious
but sexy look. It wasn't every day that you saw a man with grey eyes,
especially one whose eyes transitioned from light to dark by the
emotion he was feeling at the time. His caramel skin was so light and
smooth you would think he is a mixed breed. He had dimples that you
could sit a quarter inside, and from what I could see, he looked like he
has a nice six-pack under his shirt. He had always taken care of his
body, and I could tell he still does because his arms were well defined.
Tattoos covered his arms and neck. Oh yeah, he had a good grade of
hair that had been dreaded since we were teenagers. When he first got
his hair locked, it looked terrible because the texture of his hair was so
fine. Now, he'd had them so long I didn't think he'd look right with
anything else. He had his dreads hanging freely under a Cleveland
Cavaliers snapback, but they had grown dramatically since the last
time I saw him and were hanging mid back.

His attire was what was classified as "hood". Something so simple,
but he made it look so... damn... sexy because of his swag. Plus, he
was matching my fly in some True Religion distressed jeans, an all-
white, short-sleeved True Religion shirt, and all-white, high-top,
spiked red-bottom tennis shoes. He had an all-gold Rolex with
diamonds embedded in the links on his right wrist. On his left wrist,
he had a gold bracelet with diamonds embedded in the link. A gold
link Cuban chain with diamonds scattered throughout had the privilege of sitting on his neck. It had a charm that said *The Land*.

Once I made it back to the ER, I stopped right outside of the back
entrance and said a prayer for KJ. "Lord, please watch over KJ and

everyone in the OR with him. Lord, guide everyone's hands how you see fit. In Jesus's name, Amen!" It was in God's hands at that point.

I decided to send a group text to Camille and Moe, letting them know what happened to KJ.

**Me:** *Don't know if you've heard, but KJ was just rushed to surgery. Can't talk. At work, Sam*

I walked around the ER looking for Ben, but he was nowhere to be found, so I sent him a page letting him know what was going on.

**Camille:** *I know. I just got off the phone with D. Bitch, I'm on my way, so don't leave until I get there, Camille.*

**Me:** *OK!*

I threw my phone in my pocket so I could finish the rest of my shift, but when I made it into the break room, my phone alerted me, letting me know I had messages. When I looked at my screen, I realized it was a voicemail and text message notification from Brian. When I read the text message, it was him again with the same dance and song he did every day.

**Brian:** *Can you please call me and quit being bitter as fuck? Damn!*

After I read the text, I erased the voicemail without even listening to it because I already knew it was the same shit he sent me in a text.

This nigga had lost his total rabbit ass mind. He wanted a speedy divorce, which I was cool with, but I asked for just one thing, and he refused to give it to me. If I wanted to, I could have killed his pockets with alimony and child support because he was a surgeon, but I didn't want to because I could take care of me and Kassidy myself. I would grant him the easy divorce he wanted if he gave me the one thing I wanted for my daughter. I knew he needed to get the divorce finalized by a certain date, so I knew eventually he would see things my way.

# 2

# EARNED NOT GIVEN

Mr. Kingston James
"King"

WHEN I WAS BORN, my mother named me Kingston James, but everyone called me King. Even though I lived in the household with my mother, she didn't raise me. I ended up raising my damn self. My mother battled with drug addiction for as long as I can remember. My mother's addiction took precedence over everything in our household except her job. I'm not ashamed that she's an addict, but I am pissed at how she allowed her addiction to guide her parenting of me. If she wasn't an addict, she probably would have been a dope ass parent, but she wasn't. She's what we call a functioning dope head, and her drug of choice was and still is crack cocaine. I never met or knew much about my pops, and that's how my mother wanted it. You know how kids make up crazy ass stories? Well, mine was my father never knew I existed, and if he knew about me, he would have come in and saved me from the hell I was living. That's how I was able to cope with the situation of not having him around. It's like what child would want to walk around knowing their father didn't give a fuck about them?

My mother refused to tell me any information about my father, regardless of what I said or did. I thought about getting a private investigator involved, but I decided to let sleeping dogs lie. She said it was a one-night stand, and she never wanted me to bring him up. I knew that was a lie because over the years her story had consistently changed. The arguments surrounding it became so volatile at times between us that by the time I turned thirteen, I completely erased the thought of him from my memory bank. As far as my mother goes, I haven't spoken to her since I left for basic training two weeks after my high school graduation. She's reached out a couple of times, but I'm good with how things are. There's been too much damage done, so I've made the decision not to have her in my life, period. I'd never introduced her to KJ, and I considered her dead to me! There's no coming back from that; once I'm done, that's it.

During my junior year of high school, I decided I would join the service and serve my country. The problem is I didn't know why or how to make it happen, and it's the only out I had at the time. I didn't have schools knocking down my door because I played a sport or because I was smart like Bennie. I knew I wouldn't receive scholarships to pay for school, and truthfully, I didn't even want to go to college. But I knew that if I didn't do something by the time I graduated, I would be lost to the streets or the system. I would either be dead or in jail. I tried to stay open-minded and wait patiently for circumstances to change for me, but they never did. Like a moth to a flame, the opportunity presented itself at an end of school assembly that was held during the last class I had scheduled for the day. I was trying to get out of taking a quiz I didn't study for, and if I failed the test, I failed the class, so it was a win-win for me. During the assembly, our guidance counselors had recruiters from different careers paths speak and educate us on our options. I zeroed right in on the recruiters from the Navy, Air Force, and Army. I went over the pamphlets they gave me a million times, and I decided to go ahead and enlist with the Navy.

I dedicated my entire senior year to getting my mind and body ready. I improved my grades, worked out religiously, made healthier food choices, and anything else my recruiter suggested would give me a leg up during the selection process. After graduating from Glenville High School, I sailed through basic training, eventually morphing into a killing machine.

I wanted to continue to climb the career ladder, so I decided to apply for the Navy Seals program. The Seals are held to such a high standard that never in a million years did I think I would be selected out of all the candidates... not a raggedy kid from the slums of Cleveland, but they chose me! The training made basic training seem like a cakewalk. After the first year, I could kill someone with my bare hands, and the high I received after every kill made it so addictive. The motto to protect and serve was drilled into my brain, and I became a weapon for the United States Government.

My career was proceeding in the right direction until my team was assigned to a mission in Syria. My team took fire, and I was hit twice, but all of my team was killed with the exception of me and a guy named Devontae. We were held captive for three days while they tortured and beat the living hell out of us. The damage the bullets caused to my body was severe. The bullets penetrated my right hip and knee. I needed to had to have them both replaced with metal that I would have to walk around with for the rest of my life. The recovery process was very difficult. I had to learn how to walk again with the use of both a walker and cane. When I woke up after surgery, Tammy was sitting at my bedside with my son, who was only a couple of months old. She stayed with me for two months nursing me back to health. We flew home, and I moved in with her to finish recovering. She took care of me full time while working at Wendy's and taking college classes online. It made me look at her differently because I was able to experience the nurturing side of her, and that's when I started developing feelings for her.

About six months later, Tammy and I were still going strong, and I thought I was in love. It was right before KJ's first birthday when we found out she was pregnant again, so we went to the courthouse and got married. I didn't want to have another child brought into this world out of wedlock, so I felt it was time for me to step up and be a man for her like she stepped up for me when I needed her. Maybe a month after we tied the knot, she had a miscarriage, and from that point on, things were different.

About a year into the marriage, I started taking murder-for-hire jobs, and I got back on my feet quickly, and Tammy slowly started changing and became a person I would have never put my seed in or married willingly. It had gotten to the point where I hated going home, but KJ is the only thing that brought me home at night. Things had been crazy with us trying to make a mark in Cleveland's drug game, but she made it harder for no reason. Like the day she finally rushed KJ to the hospital. Tammy had called my phone numerous times, and I kept sending all her calls to voicemail. She constantly did that, knowing I wasn't going to answer her calls when I was out handling business. That's why I bought KJ a cell phone so he could call me himself whenever he needed something.

I was about to block her ass because she had been doing way too much for me at that point. Since I wouldn't answer, her worrisome ass started sending me text messages stating she had to rush KJ to the hospital. At first, I thought she was lying, but she sent me pictures of KJ in a hospital bed, and I knew she was telling the truth. It was sad that she lied so much that she had to send me proof of our son being in the hospital for me to believe her, but that's what had to be done, and she made it that way. I immediately stopped what I was doing and asked Damien to drive me over to the hospital. Damien is my brother from another mother, and he was also Camille's husband.

Once we made it to the ER and ran inside, the secretary directed us toward KJ's room, and as we turned the corner, I saw Tammy leaning up against the wall. She saw me and ran over to me, hugging me and placing her head on my chest. I haven't had any physical contact with her in so long that the feel of her actions was foreign. Shit like that pissed me off with her. She was always being dramatic as hell so she could get attention, or she was trying to prove to someone that we were more than what we were. I pushed her body back and looked at her like she was crazy.

"Tammy, stop fucking touching me. Where's KJ's room? He's in room four right?" As I looked up, I noticed a nurse walking out of KJ's room, and I tried to move around Tammy, but it was too late. The nurse had already walked away. I started getting angry because I wanted to talk to someone that was caring for him. I wanted to know exactly what was going on with him without all the extra stuff Tammy always added.

As I walked past her, she grabbed my shirt and pulled me back. I guess Damien lost his patience. He grabbed her hand and gently pushed her body against the wall.

"Now, bitch, I try my best to stay out of y'all shit, but you doing too fucking much right now. This man trying to make sure his seed cool, and you out here making it about you, *as always.* I suggest you walk away and give him a few minutes alone with his son before you bring your ass back into his room... Keep playing with me, and I'm going to have Camille beat your ass when she gets here. I promise you don't want those type of problems, ma!" he barked at her, then released the grip he had on her while pushing her just a little to make her stumble back.

Tammy mugged him hard, but she doesn't say one word. She knew Camille couldn't stand her ass, and she been ready to tap that ass again. Camille did it once, so I knew she wouldn't have a problem doing it again.

"Now fuck with it if you want to with your unfit ass, standing here smelling like someone just poured a bottle of liquor all over you. You should be ashamed of your fuckin' self." Dame threw out there. Tammy straightened her shirt and walked away toward the woman's bathroom.

As I walked down the hall, I just kept praying that my son would be OK over and over again. I pushed the door open, and my knees buckled from what the fuck I saw. My eyes had to be playing a trick on me because my son didn't look like this when I left that morning. KJ was laying there sweating bullets and holding his stomach, and his eyes were closed tight like he was in pain. He had a mask that was covering his nose and mouth, which I assumed giving him oxygen, and he had an IV in his arm.

I grabbed KJ's hand into my hand and started rubbing his forehead with the other hand. His forehead was hot as hell, so I assumed he had a temperature. "KJ, you OK, man?" I questioned. He opened his eyes and tears started rolling down the sides of his face. I kissed him on his forehead and sat on the edge of the bed. I kept reassuring him that he would be OK, and he was going to make it through this.

Tammy walked back into the room. She looked like she tried to pull herself together a little. I could tell she combed her hair because she pulled it up into a ponytail, and she wiped all the makeup she was wearing off of her face. She sat in a chair while remaining quiet. I just needed for someone to come in and let me know what was going on with my son.

"Can you tell me what happened between the time I left home this morning until now?" I asked Tammy in the calmest tone I could muster up.

"It's his stomach. Remember he's been having problems with it for the last couple of days, King? When I woke up, Amanda told me I should bring him in cause he's getting worse." I squinted my eyes and began rubbing my temples with my middle and index fingers due to the frustration I felt. Tammy should have been embarrassed even saying that. It was bad when the nanny had to tell you to take your child to the hospital. Two days ago, I told her to take him to see his doctor... Two fucking days ago! Tammy said when she called to schedule the appointment, the doctor said he didn't need to be seen, and it's just a stomach bug that's been going around. I felt she was lying, but I let it go because it seemed like he was getting better, and plus, I had been knee-deep in these streets.

I was about to respond to her, but the door opened, and in walked his doctor. *Muthafuckin'* Samantha Howard. She was the last person I thought would be taking care of my son. Sam was my ex and Bennie's baby sister. I hadn't seen this woman in some years, but still, when we made eye contact, it was all over for me. Within seconds, different feelings and emotions took over my mind. I think it finally registered to Sam that it was me standing there because suddenly she dropped the iPad and ran out of the room without saying a word. I picked up the iPad, inspected it briefly, and placed it on the counter.

Tammy was upset and started yelling like the ratchet bitch she was. "King, what the fuck was that about? Is she one of your hoes you fucking around on me with?" Tammy asked with an attitude and a roll of her ghetto ass neck.

"None of your damn business. Just like it ain't none of my business who you fucking *regularly*." I made it my point to emphasize the word regularly. "This about KJ, Tammy, so please don't say shit else to me unless it's about my seed." She sat back quietly, rolling her eyes at me, but I had zero fucks to give.

Someone knocked on the door, and once I told them to enter, Sam walked back into the room, and I handed over the iPad she had just dropped. She checked it for damage and once she discovered there was no damage she said, "Hello, Mr. Kingston James. I'm the doctor treating who I assume is your handsome son, KJ," Sam professionally uttered off while putting her hand out for me to shake, and I looked at her like she was crazy. Either she was trying to be professional, or she was trying to be funny because she's never called me Kingston, and when did we get on hand-shaking terms and not hugs? *She got me so fucked up right now,* I thought to myself.

I wouldn't be me if I didn't fuck with her a little. I responded, "Yes, this is my handsome son you notice he takes after his pops in the good looks department." I took a step forward so I was closer and finished, "So it's Kingston now? That's how we're doing it now, *ma*? A nigga can't get a hug or a kiss, because the last time I checked, we didn't do handshakes. Plus, I haven't seen you in quite some time," I teased, and the nervousness she was displaying made me smile because I was getting to her. She smiled, leaned in, and gave me a hug. Her perfume smelled so good... good enough to where I didn't want to let her soft ass go. I held her a few seconds longer than I should have on purpose, and then I released her from my embrace.

"Can you tell me what's going on with him? Dr. Samantha Matthews, correct?" I asked, acting like I was trying to figure out her name.

"Let me pull up his medical record real quick before I update you on what's going on with KJ," Sam responded. "So I believe KJ has something called appendicitis, which means his appendix is infected. By KJ's test results and how much pain KJ's in, I believe he needs to have surgery as soon as possible, so the doctors can remove his appendix. He should only have to stay in the hospital a couple of days after surgery, and once he's home he'll have to take it easy for a few more days, but after that he should be good as new."

"Is surgery necessary for KJ to get better?" I questioned with concern.

"Yes. If it was caught earlier, his pediatrician could have tried antibiotics first, but now he needs to have it removed. Also, while he's here, his doctor will also order for him to receive a couple of antibiotics to make sure the infection is completely gone," Sam explained further.

I gave her a sly grin that Tammy saw, and she looked up at me with the expression of *nigga, please*, but Tammy knew not to say a muthafuckin' word to me.

Before I could ask another question, the surgeons walked in, explained what was going to happen, and had me sign the consent form for KJ's surgery. Within minutes of them coming into the room, they started unhooking him from the monitors and rolled his bed out of the room. We started to pile on the elevator, and before the doors closed, Sam gave me her business card and said for me to call her if I had any questions or needed help with anything. Even with Tammy killing her with her eyes, she stayed professional and unbothered by the evil stares she was receiving.

When we got to the waiting area, the doctors told us to tell KJ bye. Tammy kissed him on the forehead and walked into the waiting room.

"KJ, I love you, son, so much, and I'll see you after the doctors fix your stomach so it's not hurting anymore. OK, big man?" He nodded his head up and down, I kissed him once more and walked into the waiting room myself.

"Is something going on I need to know about? I see your burner jumping, and you kept stepping out into the hall to hold conversations privately downstairs. What's up? My phone hasn't rang once, so I assume you told Keys to block my calls and send messages and calls to just you and Bennie. Come on and tell daddy what's wrong," I asked fuckin' with Dame. We both started chuckling louder than we intended because a few people looked over our way.

"Main called me and said he feels Chris has been moving funny, and when he went to get the money bag today to deliver to the Hubb it felt lite. He and Dolla Bill counted the money separately with a counter, and they came up with the same total. The bag was short ten thousand dollars," Dame said lowly so no one could hear what he was saying.

"We'll deal with Chris later, but have Keys go over the footage from that house for the last week, and tell her to pay close attention to Chris and how he's moving. Also, have her place videos in his apartment. Lately, he's been rubbing me the wrong way, and I feel like something's going on. I've had him securing and driving Tammy around to this last week to watch her ass because I feel like she's up to something. He's been reporting back that he hasn't seen shit out of the norm, but I feel like that's a lie." He nodded his head, letting me know he would take care of it.

"Did you know Sam was back in town?" Dame asked.

A smile graced my face when I thought of Sam. "Yeah. This my first time seeing Sam's fine, thick ass. Bennie told me she came back, but it slipped my mind until she walked into KJ's room."

"Damn, nigga. What the fuck you smiling so hard for? You do know she's married, right! You know she'll never cheat on that nigga either 'cause she ain't built like that. Plus, she's pregnant again... You ready to play stepdaddy to two kids, nigga?" He started laughing like what he said was really funny. He always trying to crack jokes, but his jokes was corny as *fuck*. I stood to walk away because I needed to get away from this nigga before I punched him in his face. Sam had always been a soft spot for me, and he knew that. Yes, I still cared about Sam. Shit, honestly, I'd probably always care about her. So, *no*, I didn't want to hear about her fucking another nigga, even if it was her husband.

"Ha, ha, ha! Nigga, sit your whipped ass down. You ain't even had a taste of the pussy in over a decade, and you ready to shoot a nigga in the head." I wanted to give him some real facts, but I let the shit go, especially with so many people ear hustlin' in that muthafucka. For example, this white lady that was sitting across the room looked over at me and Dame. Her ass was ear hustlin' like a muthafucka, but I ignored her and continued talking to Dame

"Has Bennie said anything to you pertaining to why all of a sudden she decided to come back here to live? For her to get a job here means she's trying to put down roots," Dame asked.

"Nah, he just told me she was moving back. Why, did he say something to you about her?"

"No, he hasn't said anything to me. But I did overhear a lot of Camille's one-sided conversations she's constantly having with Sam. Dude did some foul shit to her, and that's why she decided to move back and divorce his dumb ass. Sam, Kassidy, and her babysitter moved back here. But for real though, leave baby sis alone with your thirsty ass, nigga… On a serious note though, Sam did tell Camille she doesn't want that type of relationship with you. She said she don't mind being friends, but that's as far as she wants it to go, and I heard that from her mouth when Mill had her on speaker one day. Plus, you know Bennie's going to have a problem with y'all doing anything, especially since you're both married, and Tammy ain't going nowhere no time soon. And nigga, you owe my wife a nice ass gift because she had your back and told Sam she thinks y'all should get back together because y'all good together." I began really thinking about what D said, and he was right. I was going to let Sam be because I had too much going on myself.

"That's why Mill, baby sis because she has my back at all times, and she goes hard in the paint for me. She'll drop a bitch where she stands if I asked her to and without question. I got her though, just as soon as shit dies down a little."

We sat around for maybe three hours talking and joking, and suddenly, Damien stood and dapped me up. "I'm about to run over to the spot on Parkgate real quick and see what's shakin'. Call and let me know how my lil' nigga doin'. Oh yeah, Camille texted me a few minutes ago, letting me know she's on her way here." I said okay, and as Damien began walking toward the entrance, KJ's surgeons walked into the waiting area. Damien turned and walked back over to where I was standing. We all braced ourselves for what the doctor was about to say.

The look the surgeon gave me before he started explaining everything caused a chill to run down my spine. Tammy walked up next to me and grabbed my hand. For some odd reason, I allowed her to and didn't pull my hand back. I guess because something just didn't feel right.

"Can you please follow me to the surgery consultation room? I would like to discuss KJ's condition with you." I nodded, and we followed his lead. We piled into the room, but we all stayed standing, looking around nervous as hell.

The surgeon looked me in the eyes and stated, "Mr. and Mrs. James, when we opened your son up, we realized his appendix had already ruptured or burst. The infection spread throughout his body, causing him to become septic, which means the infection spread throughout his body by mode of his blood. The infection caused KJ's heart to stop while we were in the OR. We were able to get it restarted and stabilize him enough to finish the surgery. We've started him on an additional antibiotic to help with the infection, and at this time, we don't know the exact extent of damage the infection has caused to his body, but we're optimistic that he'll pull through and make a complete recovery. He's currently on his way up to the ICU as we speak, and I'll escort you guys up there," the surgeon explained.

"How long will he be in the hospital, and is he out of the woods?" I asked.

"Well, you know kids bounce back from things quicker than adults, so probably a week or so. We put him in the ICU so he can be watched carefully, and if something happens, we'll be there to catch it quickly. We also decided to keep the breathing tube in for a couple of days and to keep Kingston slightly sedated so his body doesn't have to work so hard to heal." After we finished talking with the surgeon, he escorted us to the ICU to see KJ.

Once I saw he was OK, I decided to go handle the business I was in the process of handling back at the Hubb when Tammy called me earlier. I hated leaving my son there, but some things just couldn't be helped, especially because we were in the middle of revamping our organization.

We all had our parts to play as founders. Bennie handled the purchase, production, and enhancements of the legal drugs our organization sold illegally. Damien handled the purchasing and selling of our weapons. I took care of purchasing the illegal drugs we sold and maintained and ran our legal businesses, amongst other things, and we all handled the distribution aspect of our organization.

Man, it hadn't been easy in the least developing the foundation we needed to allow our business to thrive and possibly expand, but it was necessary, so the three of us put in the work needed to make things happen. If things worked out how we planned them to, in the next two years, the three of us would be the only plugs for the East Coast. Looking back over the last five years, we worked our asses off getting KDB off the ground, and our success wasn't handed to us like some. We had to put our blood, sweat, and tears into the business, and everything we had at that point was earned, not given.

# 3

# MY TRUTH

## MRS. MONIQUE HOWARD

### "Moe"

MONIQUE HOWARD IS what my parents named me, but everyone called me Moe, and I was Bennie's better half. I was born and raised in Atlanta, Georgia, but I currently reside in Cleveland, Ohio with my husband. I'm a simple, southern girl to heart, so it was kind of hard adjusting to this fast-paced city living when I moved here. My parents have been together and married for over thirty years, and I'm proud to say they're still madly in love with each other. They loved each other's stankin' drawers, so it was none of that fake bullshit Bennie's parents portrayed over the years. Those are some relationship goals for that ass, and I pray we make it that far and hopefully beyond.

My father played for the NFL for over ten years. He played for multiple teams throughout his career; The Browns, The Hawks, and The Dolphins just to name a few. About ten years ago, my father opened a sports agency that's based out of Atlanta, and it is one of the top sports agencies worldwide. My mother owns an upscale all-service salon where she provided services to a long list of VIP clientele.

My parents had always been very successful in their own right.

They came from the slums but used the opportunities allotted to them to make them successful. Both of my parents received college degrees and pushed me extremely hard, almost too hard at times, to get good grades. That was how I ended up at Howard. That was their alma mater, and they refused to pay for me to go to any other university. I can't be too mad because that's where I met my arrogant, six-foot, dark-chocolate, bald-headed king with a long ass beard that I could actually pull.

We met during a physiology class that we were both enrolled in while attending Howard. Our professor coupled the two of us up for an assignment we had to present together. Up until that point, I had never really paid any attention to him, but all that changed when we met up at Starbucks to work on the joint assignment. The more we worked together, the more attracted to him I became, and we've been together ever since.

It was sad to say that the culture I grew up in found no value in a girl or woman maintaining their virginity until marriage, but that's because people changed sex partners like they changed underwear. My so-called "friends" in high school would say I thought my pussy was made of gold and better than theirs, which at times made me question if I was doing the right thing by not having sex. Due to all the teasing I was receiving, it caused my boyfriend to break up with me because he said I was acting like an immature child. Ain't that some shit?

My mother raised me to believe my pussy was a gift, and any man I decided to allow a taste had to earn the privilege of having me. That's why it took me six months for me to have sex with Bennie, and up until right before he penetrated me, he had no clue I was a virgin. I thought if I told him I never had sex, he wouldn't want to be with me, but it was the complete opposite. He took his time with my body making sure I felt so much pleasure. He showed so much patience while teaching me how to please him, and it truly was magical, and it made me love and appreciate him even more.

The values my mother instilled in me, such as self-worth, and confidence, integrity, and fidelity, are some of the things I planned on passing down to my daughter. The values we shared are the things that drew Bennie and I closer together because we shared the same values regarding marriage and the roles of the husband and wife in a marriage. We felt the man's place was at the head of his household, and a woman's place was to raise the kids and make sure the household is running smoothly. Because we shared those values, it made transitioning from boyfriend and girlfriend to husband and wife easier.

Bennie had no problem with me working as long as the home front is taken care of. When I gave birth to our first child, Bennett Jr., I decided to quit working and became a stay-at-home mom. Bennie and I had two children, Bennett Jr., but we all called him BJ, and Jessica together, who we all called Jess.

I thought I knew love when I got with Bennie, but when I found out I was pregnant with BJ, everything changed for me. What drove my decision to be a stay-at-home mom is my upbringing. With my father being in the NFL, he was always out of town for work, so it was really just me and my mom. Being a hairstylist meant she held long hours, and when she would get home, she would be exhausted. So needless to say, my grandmother raised me with the help of my mother. That was something I didn't want for my children. I knew their father had an exhausting career, and I wanted to make up for him not being there as much as I could. The things that seemed important when we first got married weren't in that moment.

I worked up until I delivered BJ, and I told my boss when I left to go on maternity leave, it was a chance I may not come back. After I had my baby, every time I thought about going back to work, I would have panic attacks, so Bennie supported me not working. Being a good mother and wife became my full-time job that I took very seriously. Waking them up in the mornings, giving them baths, helping them with homework, and putting them to bed gave me life. I do know if I ever decided to work outside the home again, Bennie would support my decision.

When my youngest was six, I was involved in a fatal car accident, and I had a lot of trouble coping after I healed, so my therapist suggested volunteering abroad because it helped a few of her patients with their depression. Initially, I was reluctant and only contributed financially, but eventually, I had a chance to go abroad, and it was amazing, and I've been hooked ever since.

The program I traveled with went to different countries, mostly Africa, helping women and children of domestic abuse, rape, trauma, and mutilation caused by violence. We offered the women and children shelter, food, clothing, medical treatment, and therapy just to name a few things. Our goal was to help the women get past the trauma caused to their minds and bodies after being brutally attacked.

I helped me with me my depression and anxiety, but it also hurt my marriage because Bennie didn't understand how me volunteering helped me be at peace with my past. Bennie got fed up and threatened me with divorce if I didn't come home, so I had been back home from my last stent of volunteering for approximately a month, and things between Bennie and I still was in a bad place. Tension was heavy between the two of us, and I knew things wasn't going to get better unless I opened up to my husband and told him the truth about everything... *my truth.*

It was sad that my husband had to threaten me with divorce for me to see how broken things were between the two of us. He really didn't have to threaten me because I had already decided I wasn't going back abroad when I came home anyway. It was time for me to stop running away from my problems and face them head-on. I knew how hard things were for him when I left, but I was being selfish and just thinking about myself, but now that was over.

While volunteering, some days were way harder than others, and at times, it was tough staying motivated, but I knew I had to stick it out. I felt like volunteering was something God guided me to do, but the downfall to that was, my marriage suffered from being away from home so much, and I didn't know if we could recover from all the damage that had been done. But one thing was for sure, I knew that I wanted my marriage, but our problems ran deep... so deep that I had to set an appointment for me and Bennie to see our family therapist.

Since I had been home, we had been sleeping separately with me in the master bedroom, and Bennie was sleeping in one of the guest bedrooms. It had gotten to the point that I couldn't sit in through another meaningless conversation with Bennie. We didn't really address any issues we were having, and we ended up blaming each other for things and arguing.

On top of everything else, intimacy had become nonexistent between us, and it was killing my horny ass. Normally, we couldn't keep our hands off each other and would end up fucking all over the house, but we hadn't had sex at that point in a little over five months, so I was desperate to have sex with my husband and release some of this sexual tension I had. Horny wasn't a strong enough word to describe how I was feeling. I felt manic at that point. If Bennie was to blow on my ear, I promise you I would have had multiple orgasms, back-to-back. It took everything in me not to go in his room and rape him at night, but I felt like sex wouldn't do anything but confuse what we're going through even more.

That's why when he was on his way out of the door, I acted like I was sleeping when he peeked his head into my room. Right before he pulled out the driveway, he sent me a text message letting me know he had left for work. I knew I had to pull my shit together before I lost my husband, so it was time I pulled my big-girl panties up and handled business.

I decided to just get up and get my day started because I knew there was no way I could go back to sleep. I rolled over in my comfortable Serta Comfort mattress, taking in all of its comforts. Other than my family, I think I missed my bed the most while traveling because in Africa, I was sleeping on a hard ass cot every night.

I grabbed my phone off my nightstand and slowly sat up in the middle of the bed and crossed my legs Indian style. As I scrolled through my contacts, I stopped once I saw my husband's name. I touched the screen, and the phone dialed his number. The phone rang five times, and then it went to voicemail, and without leaving a message, I hung up. I opened our text thread and sent him a text about us meeting up for lunch. He texted back for me to meet him at his office at twelve-thirty, which I was fine with.

I really hoped he hadn't been out here being unfaithful, but in a way, it was hard to be mad if he was because I neglected my wifely duties badly. But I refused to drive myself crazy wondering what he was doing every second of the day while I was away. I had noticed since I had returned home that something or someone had him shook because he was moving funny to me. I threw my phone on the bed and headed to the bathroom so I could get my day started.

After I took my shower, I walked into my closet to find something sexy but still classy to wear because I had to be on point going to my husband's job. I decided to intentionally not wear a bra on my 36C breasts, but I did put on a pair of all-black, lace boy shorts. I found one of Bennie's all-white button-down shirts that stopped about two inches above my knees. I rolled the sleeves up to my elbows, and some black-and-white checkered peep-toed, five-inch red bottom that Bennie bought me and I'd been dying to wear. I applied a thin, natural beat to my caramel skin, a red-tinted lip gloss, untwisted my natural hair that fell a little past my shoulders, grabbed the matching purse to my shoes and my aviator Ray-Ban sunglasses, and headed downstairs to leave. As I walked past the full-length mirror in the foyer, I stopped and took in my appearance. I felt I accomplished the sexy but classy look I was going for, and I looked damn good wearing it.

It was a little after eleven-thirty by the time I got in my 2017 all-white Porsche Cayenne. I connected my phone to my car's Bluetooth, started my Apple Music playlist, and pulled out my driveway. As I drove through traffic, a call came through. The caller ID said Mr. David Thomas. David is the man that ran the program I volunteered with that went abroad. I didn't even want to answer it, but I knew I had to get it over with and tell him I was done going abroad. He was going to be upset because I played a pivotal role in the organizing and success of our trips, but I had to put my family first.

"Answer call." The Bluetooth picked up, and the bass in his voice boomed through my speakers. I answered dryly, trying not to leave room for him to think shit was sweet. This is a straight-professional relationship for me, but I thought somewhere things got blurred for him.

"Hey, Moe, this David... I want to know if we can get together and start the planning for the next trip abroad. I want to get your input regarding the different programs we could offer this time when we go. Maybe we can grab some lunch and discuss everything. What you think?"

"David, I'm sorry to tell you this, but I won't be going abroad with you guys this time, maybe never again. I really enjoyed the experience over the last two years, but I have neglected my own family in the attempt of trying to help others. I can't do it anymore. I'm sorry but not sorry."

The line went silent, and I thought David had hung up, but when I looked at the screen on the dash, the call was still connected, so I knew he hadn't.

"Moe, why? Wait, does this have anything to do with what happened the night before we came back to the States? I told you I'm sorry, and I wish I could take it back because things have been different between the two of us ever since. I misjudged things, and I'm not going to lie... I do have strong feelings for you, but I would never want to come between you and your husband. I thought you were giving me signs that you felt the same, but I guess I misjudged things. Again, I'm sorry Moe, but don't make the women and children pay for my sins. These women really need you."

I knew the women we helped needed as much support as they could get, but someone else would have to give them that. My family needed me way more than those women did.

He had me questioning my actions because I did try to keep things as professional as possible, but there were times when we confided in and leaned on each other during our difficult times there. David and I would talk for hours about stuff. We even talked about our spouses. It was so easy for me to talk to David. I think it had a lot to do with him never judging me regardless of what I told him.

"If I did things to make you feel that way, I also apologize. The support you and the others gave me while traveling is very much appreciated. We're both married, and we were wrong to allow things to even get the point that it did get to. Let's chalk it up to us both missing our spouses and that's it. Leave that shit in Africa because all it can do is cause problems. You know me well enough to know I won't do shit to jeopardize that. On top of that, you know my husband's batshit crazy, and if he thought something was going on, he'd kill both of us. I just believe it's time to cut ties. I have no problem helping with events and volunteering here in the States. I'll hold down things here while you're gone" The line went silent again. I knew he had feelings for me, but I would have never disrespected my husband in that way.

"Moe, you're an amazing woman, and your husband is one lucky man. If this was a different lifetime, I think we would be awesome together." He chuckled softly, and I smiled. "We were friends before I complicated things, and I would like to continue being friends. But I want to ask this question as your friend, have you talked to Bennie about what happened?" I had to turn down a side street and pull over. Once I safely pulled over, I put the car in park and just thought about it all.

"No," I softly answered. "I know it's time for me to talk to my husband. At this point, if I don't, we're going to end up divorced, and I don't want that. Every time I get ready to tell him I back out because that means I have to relive everything that happened back then, and that's a hard pill for me to swallow." The tears began falling, and I mean to the point where my thighs were wet.

"Monique, I know it was hard, but you've made so much progress since then. You're ready to get your marriage back on track, and I think now is the time to do it. The first step is telling your husband everything. If you trust him with your heart, you should trust him with your truth. Go talk to him and let me know how it goes, OK?" David wisely said. See what I mean when I said he was so easy to talk to.

"I'm on my way to his office now, and I'm going to put everything on the table. I've been back a month, and every time I try to talk to him, something comes up, or I get scared shitless and put telling him off. If I don't do it now, I don't think we'll ever have this discussion. Thanks, David. I'll shoot you a text later. Maybe we can meet up sometime next week, and I can help you plan the trip." The phone hung up before he could respond.

Before I could pull back into traffic good, the phone rang again. I immediately hit the answer button thinking it was David. *"Friend,* did you forget to say something?" I asked, smiling.

"Hello, Monique, this is Dr. Agarwall. I hope I didn't catch you at a bad time. How have you and the family been doing since you've been home? I know everyone's excited about you being home. I called last night, but you didn't answer, so I decided to give you a try now."

"We're all doing good. I'm trying to get things back on track with my husband, but I can't complain. So what's up, Dr. Agarwall?" I inquired.

"I was calling with the results of the biopsy we took right before you left Africa." Damn, I had been dealing with so much that the biopsy results completely slipped my mind.

"OK, the password is Bennett; you can go ahead and give me the results."

"Well, Monique, the results show... the treatment you went through worked, and you should be able to get pregnant now. I'm so happy for you, Monique. But even though we got these results, we're not done yet, missy. So don't think you're getting rid of me that easily. We're not done until you and Bennett are able to hold a bundle of joy in your arms again. I still want to follow-up with you next month. I'll be in the States in a month, and you can come to my clinic to get checked out if that's OK with you. Considering you're the first woman that has had these positive results, I'm willing to travel to you and continue with the treatment needed. I know your husband is going to be so happy, Monique. I'm so happy for you both, sweetheart."

"Oh my Godddd! Yes! I'll be there with bells on. Have your assistant send me an email with the location, time, and date. Hopefully, when I come, I'll already be pregnant; cross your fingers, Dr. Agarwall. Again, thank you again soooo much."

I had been waiting over two years to hear that woman tell me the treatment worked. If I didn't have the courage before, I had the courage now. I had to tell Bennie everything so he would really understand why I had done the things I had done over the last couple of years. I wasn't running from my husband; I was running from my past mistakes. I just sat there in the car for ten minutes crying and thanking God. I looked up in the rearview mirror, and my damn foundation and eyeliner were running down my face, so I grabbed a baby wipe out of the glove compartment to clean my face. I wiped all the makeup off and applied some lotion on my face because it was dry as hell. I started my car back up and continued on to my destination.

Let me explain, after we had our second child, Jessica, Bennie and I both wanted at least two more children, so we started trying when our daughter turned six months. We were having trouble initially, but our doctors reassured us that nothing was wrong. Right before Bennie's mother died about two and a half years ago, I found out I was pregnant again, and we were both ecstatic. It was short-lived though because when Ma Howard, or Renee, died, Bennie started spiraling out of control badly.

He was diagnosed with depression by Dr. Kelly Winters. She prescribed him some medication, but he refused to take the shit. Man, that was such a hard time for us both, and I honestly didn't think our marriage would survive it. Bennie was acting crazy and reckless out here in these streets—drinking, smoking, beating and shooting people in broad daylight, and what did it for me is when he came home covered in blood refusing to tell me where it came from.

I was so busy trying to protect and help him through his shit that I started losing myself piece by piece. I ended up having a bad car accident, and mentally, I couldn't take the outcome of the fatal accident and ended up depressed and suicidal. That's one of the reasons I started volunteering abroad so I could help others and forget about my problems.

After telling you guys all that, finally, I have the courage to tell y'all my secret. Someone close to us... raped me, and the rape was brutal. That's not the worse part though. When I was able to finally get away from that bitch after he raped me, I jumped in my car and dashed out of there trying to get away. While driving, I passed out and wrapped my car around a telephone pole. When I was rushed to the emergency room, I was told that I suffered a miscarriage due to the trauma from the rape and the accident.

The doctors rushed me into surgery before Bennie arrived, so I was able to put my medical information on lock, and I told Bennie what I wanted him to know. I told him about me being infertile and the miscarriage. It made him snap out of whatever mental shit he was going through to take care of me, the roles reversed because he was so worried about me. He became my muthafuckin' rock in many ways. He catered to my every want and need, but the loss of a child is something that's irreplaceable. Even though he waited on me around the clock, he couldn't do anything about to internal battle I was having with myself. To know you're the reason your child died is a hard pill to swallow. I contemplated suicide multiple times for months, but I couldn't be that selfish and take my own life. Plus, I felt like it was a good reason why God spared my life the day I had the accident.

I finally pulled up to the entrance of Cleveland Clinic and cut the car off. I just needed to sit there for a minute and collect my thoughts. Within seconds, the valet attendant knocked on my window, and she asked, "Hello. I'm Toni Roberson. Would you like to park valet today?"

"Yes," I answered. I handed her my keys, and she gave me a parking ticket. I grabbed our food I picked up from Grum's Sandwich Shop on Coventry and started the long ass walk to his office. I ain't going to lie… If I felt I could have pushed the conversation back and have it later when Bennie got home, I would've. I just knew if I didn't go through with it then, I would lose my nerve again, and I had to get this shit off my chest because it was eating me alive.

I began the long journey walking from the hospital's entrance over to the emergency department, where Bennie's office was located. I noticed they had put two new stores inside of the atrium— Starbucks and a high-end gift shop. It took me twenty minutes of nonstop walking until I stepped off the elevator on his floor. I should have gone inside that gift shop and bought me some flat shoes, *shit*. My fucking feet were hurting bad as hell, and I knew better than to wear those five-inch heels when I put them on. My feet hurt so bad they felt like they were about to fall off at any moment. I swear if I was anywhere else, I would have taken my shoes off and walked barefoot.

"Hey, Cindy, is Bennett in his office?" I asked his secretary because when I walked up, I noticed his office door was closed.

She looked up at me and smiled before standing and giving me a big hug. "Hey, Moe!" she screamed excitedly. "I didn't know you were back. How long have you been back?" she screamed in my ear, and then she released me out of her grasp. Your big-headed husband didn't say anything." She walked back around her desk and took a seat back her office chair.

"About a month, but I've been getting acclimated back to my life here, so it had been impossible for me to make my way down here. Sorry, Cindy."

"Well, I'm glad you're back because Ben has been running himself ragged, trying to keep his head above water. He's been dealing with a lot, but I'm pretty sure you already know that."

"We're supposed to be having lunch!" I raised the bag of food so she could see it. "Is it OK for me to go in his office, or is he in the middle of a meeting or something?" Cindy gave me a look like *bitch, please*, so I knew she was about to tell me what was on her mind.

"He's in his office talking to Diane. You can go in." She gave me another funny look because she couldn't stand Diane, and every chance Cindy got, she let her know. Cindy's white ass was too old to be messy like that, but hey, to each its own. "Oh, yeah, warning! Watch her ass, and that's all I'm going to say." She didn't even have to say that much because I was already hip to the game, and I had been watching her ass since she started there. I been told Bennie she had a thing for him, but he always brushed it off like I was being extra. I knew my husband would never cross the line with her, but she wasn't about to be disrespectful to me either.

I walked up to the door and knocked, waiting for my invitation to enter, and when Bennie told me to come in, I did just that. For some reason, this bitch Diane mugged the fuck out of me, and I mean, she mugged me hard. She tried to clean it up though before I noticed, but it was too late. We've never had a problem before, so I didn't know why she was throwing me shade.

"Hey, *wife*." Bennie gave me his award-winning smile, showing all his white teeth. "I'm so sorry the time got away from me. You look beautiful, mama!" Bennie was smiling from ear to ear. He walked over to me, looked me up and down, licked his juicy ass lips, and gave me a hug and a nice, sensual kiss on the lips. That was the most affection I had received from him since I had been back home, so again, I was a little caught off guard. But I kissed him back, and then it deepened it a little, but we quickly pulled back when Diane cleared her throat, and we both turned and looked at her.

"Sorry about that, Diane. Can we finish this conversation later on when I come down to the ER? I have a few things I need to check on before I leave for the day. I'll page you when I'm on my way down there so you can give me your specific location.

"Also, make sure you send me an email letting me know if and how you figure out the staffing problem we're facing tonight. I think it may be a good idea to have a few agency nurses cover the schedule for tonight and tomorrow. Just send me an email letting me know how you decide to handle things," he stated while never breaking eye contact with me. I could see so much lust in his eyes that I got uncomfortable, and I had to look away.

"Let me get out of here," Diane said with an attitude and a roll of her neck. "Monique, it was good to see you again. Bennie never mentioned that you were back. Bennie I'll text or call you tonight, and let you know if our *little* problem has been taken care of," Diane said while she grabbed her things and stepped around us and tried to exit, but I stepped in front of her quickly to bring her steps to a halt. Now I could have read into her comment and checked this bitch real hard regarding the "little problem" comment, but I refused to let her know she got under my skin. But what I was going to address was the professional disrespect she was displaying.

"No, you won't call, Dr. Howard, but what you will do is as he asked, which is send him an email explaining the resolution you come up with regarding staffing." Once I finished, I moved to the side so she could walk out, which she did, but not before slamming the door behind her.

"Does she have a problem that needs to be addressed, because I'm trying to figure out why she mugging me, *husband*?" I sarcastically questioned. I sat the bag of food and my purse on the small, round table in his office. As I started setting our lunch up for us, Bennie walked up behind me and pulled me into a bear hug from the back, and my body melted right into his because it felt so good.

He kissed me on the back of my neck, released me, and then walked around the table and took a seat. "I have no idea why she mugged you, but we're all stressed about the bullshit going on, so maybe it was just that. Hell, I don't know," he said while shrugging his shoulders. I took my seat, and he held his hands out with the palms facing up. I placed my hands in his, and we bowed our heads, and he led us in prayer, praying over our lunch, health, and marriage. Man, I was so in awe of this man and how far he had come.

"You know last night I did a lot of praying and soul-searching, and I came to the conclusion that I want my marriage, and I want to do anything I can to make our reconciliation happen. This morning, it took everything in me not to come into our bedroom and make love to my beautiful wife. The only thing that stopped me was, I knew we needed to discuss some things before we could be intimate again. Moe, we both have made a ton of mistakes in the last couple of years, but right now is the time to for you to let me in so we can work out our problems together. I want to give you the floor to tell me how you feel with no judgment. I promise."

Once I swallowed the food in my mouth and took a swig of Diet Pepsi, I began. "This is going to be hard for me, so please be patient with me, Bennie, so I can get it all out." He nodded his head this time, letting me know he understood.

"Well, first I want to say I love you with all my heart, and I want our marriage to work." I looked down at my hands, rubbing them together feverishly. "First of all, I want to thank you for always supporting me and taking care of the home front by yourself for the last two years. Helping those women and children helped me in more ways than you could ever imagine. I felt like the women could relate to me better than anyone because we had gone through similar things. With the help of the therapist, I've developed tools to help me when I'm going through tough times." The tears started flowing, and the more tears that rolled down my face, the more comfortable I felt telling Bennie about what happened. I grabbed a couple of tissues out of the Kleenex box so I could wipe away the tears. I sat back down so I could continue with my truth. "So…um…when I had the car accident, it was a few things I left out of the story. The reason I passed out while driving is because I had been beaten repeatedly in the head. That's why I lost consciousness." I cleared my throat and looked down at my hands that were resting in my lap.

"Moe, keep going, baby. I got you, ma." My husband walked over to me, grabbed my hands, and pulled me up from the chair and into his lap. He wrapped his arms around me and rested his head on the top of my head oh so tenderly. "Moe, go ahead and finish. I got you, ma."

"OK. Well… right before I jumped into the car and had the accident, I was brutally beat and raped. The blows I took to my head is what caused me to pass out while driving and wrap my car around a telephone pole. Baby, I'm so sorry, Bennie. The accident was all my fault, and I should have just stopped when I was a safe distance away, pulled over, and called the police." At that point, my whole body was shaking in his lap, and I broke down sobbing, completely losing it. He pulled my body in tightly and began to rub my back, rocking us both back and forth in a soothing manner. I used to rock him back and forth like that when he would wake up in the middle of the night from a nightmare in college.

Even though I was upset, it felt like a big weight had been lifted off my shoulders by telling him that. I knew I was not off the hook yet because I knew he was about to ask the million-dollar question next. This is why I had been running from the truth for the last two years because I didn't want to tell him who raped me.

It took me about a good five minutes to calm down and relax enough to continue. He didn't say anything, which was odd, but it caused the wheels in my head to start turning. He had to know because he wasn't flipping out. "You already knew about the rape, didn't you?" I asked slightly above a whisper. Instead of answering the question, he hugged me tighter and started avoiding eye contact. Eventually, he looked down into my eyes. When we made eye contact, the tears from his eyes dropped and rolled down his face. That made me sadder because this man was hurting because of my hurt that was caused by what someone else did to me. That's love.

"Yeah, I found out a couple of months ago. I was doing some research regarding the infertility problems we're having. I looked at your medical record and read the notes from the surgeon that did your DNC and fixed all the internal injuries you had. I was mad as fuck, and believe me, until I calmed down, a few people lost their lives. I think I was more angry at that point because I didn't know who did it. I feel like I wasn't there to protect you, and that shit is eating me up. I was so busy being selfish as fuck and acting crazy because my mother died. It allowed someone an opening to come in and hurt you. I just wish you would have told me so I could get you the help you needed. I was there to help you with the physical, but I checked out on you mentally." He pecked my lips a couple of times oh so gently. That action alone brought me so much comfort.

"I didn't say anything because I didn't want you to go off the deep end again. You were just getting over the effects your mother's death had on you. I just couldn't add to that." Bennie sighed heavily, and then he released his arms from around my body.

"There's more. Initially, I lied about my intentions when I went abroad the first time. The first time I went abroad it was so I could be part of a research program that aided in the strengthening of a woman's uterus and cervix by way of medication, making the probability of maintaining the pregnancy increase by 75%. I did volunteer alongside the church, but I also was being treated by their therapist in an attempt to get myself together mentally. When Dr. Agarwall and David saw how well my mind and body responded to both programs, we collectively decided to combine the programs.

"I got a call from Dr. Agarwall on my way here stating the results from the biopsy I took before I left shows that the treatments I received were successful. That means that I should be able to get pregnant now and carry to full term. I was so excited when she told me the news, but after divulging everything, it was making me second-guess everything." I couldn't think straight with him all over me, so I got up and took a seat on the top of his mahogany desk. It really was a waste of me moving because he came and stood between my legs and wrapped his arms around me pulling my face into his chest kissing the top of my head. I wrapped my arms around him, closed my eyes, and took in his scent. My body relaxed, and it made me realize that he was home for me, and I didn't think any man could ever give me that, but I knew it was the calm before the storm because when I revealed my rapist, he was going to go apeshit.

"Do you feel the therapy you received helped with the depression you were dealing with when you first left to go abroad?" Bennie lifted my chin and placed a nice and gentle kiss on my lips. Intimate moments like that was what I cherished and craved, and I wanted that the rest of my life.

"Yes, I believe it helped me. The therapist helped me develop tools to use when I feel like I'm drowning. Also, this last time, we were able to get a therapist that specializes in treating patients struggling with grief after the loss of a loved one. The loss of children is something hard for anyone to deal with mentally. But when you combine the rape and me being the one behind the wheel of the car, it had me ready to take my life. My therapist felt I need to be completely transparent with you and let you know how bad the depression was." I could feel his energy shift because of what I had just said about taking my life. I wasn't going to lie because I was really in bad headspace, but I was better.

I looked up, and we made eye contact. "Baby, you don't have to worry about me. If I ever feel like life's not worth living, I will tell you so you can get me some help. I promise I'm good." We silently stared at each other, and I already knew he was looking for any hint of doubt that I was lying or unsure.

"Since Dr. Agarwall said the treatment was successful, do you feel now's a good time for us to even be thinking about having another child?" Bennie asked.

"Honestly, I don't know. Yes, I do want more children, but it was not fair to bring them into this world when we truly don't know where things lie with our marriage. I ain't going to lie... When you mentioned divorce, it lit a fire under my ass to get my shit together. But one thing for sure, and two things are certain: I'll never willingly sign divorce papers, and I'll appreciate it if you never threaten me again with it. I think we should leave it in God's hands by not using protection, and if He sees fit for us to have another child, it will happen. I want us to go to couple's therapy and keep repairing our relationship that we both played a part in damaging."

He grabbed my face with both hands and kissed my forehead, my nose, and then my lips softly, barely making contact. "I want to apologize for threatening to divorce you. I could never do that shit. I love you too much, Ma. I was so fucking desperate to get you back home to me that I was willing to do or say anything that would make that happen."

The way this man was looking into my eyes was making me feel like he could see into my fuckin' soul. The lust was so evident, but he was battling with his conscience on whether to make a sexual advance, or if he should wait until he knew I was definitely better. but how I was feeling, I was down to fuck right then and there.

He broke our silence. "Damn, I love your sexy ass... and it is taking everything in me not to fuck you on my desk right now." He leaned in so our foreheads were resting on one another, and seconds later, he started tonguing me down. We both got lost in the moment, and I honestly forgot we were at his office. His hands roamed my body feverishly, and he lightly brushed his thumbs against my nipples every time his hands rubbed over my breasts. A small moan escaped my mouth, and my pussy started thumping hard as hell... so hard that it felt like the beat could be heard out loud. *I'm so horny*, I thought to myself, and I swear at that moment I could have cried.

Bennie suddenly pulled his body away from in between my legs, and he took a seat on the arm of the chair right in front of his desk.

All the good energy my husband was previously giving me was gone, and it was replaced with coldness. He looked me in the eyes, and I already knew what time it was.

"Monique, I need a name."

Even though I knew he was about to ask me that question, it still made me nervous when the words crossed his lips. I didn't want to answer the question. I wished I could get out of answering the question. I stayed silent because those three letters are going to rock my husband to the core.

"Monique!" I jumped because of how loud he yelled my name.

Tears began to cascade down my face, and my body started trembling. I was thinking that at any minute he was going to come over and show me some comfort, but no, not at all. For some reason, it made me angry. I wiped the tears, grabbed my purse, and headed for the door. Before I could walk out of the door I let him know the answer to his question.

"It was your father, Max, who raped me!"

# 4

# TIME OF DEATH

## DR. BENNETT HOWARD

### "Bennie"

I JUST KEPT REPLAYING the conversation my wife and I had before she left. I had been sitting there thinking about the different things she said he did to her and of all the things she didn't say.

*"It was your father, Max, who raped me!" Moe yelled at me. She opened the door so she could leave, but I stopped her before she could completely make it out of the door. I pulled her back in my office and shut the door.*

*"What happened? If you don't want to tell me, I understand," I asked softly and in a controlled manner because I didn't want her to think I was upset with her. If she thought I was upset, she would shut down altogether, and I wanted her to divulge what happened in its entirety. On the other hand, silently, I was praying she was at a place where she didn't want to relive the hurtful ordeal because I didn't know if I could really handle hearing how the sick bastard violated her. I could feel her body slightly stiffen, and then she started shaking uncontrollably. I placed my hand to the back of her neck and pulled her lips toward mine. I kissed her lips softly in an attempt to relax her, and after a few light pecks, she relaxed some.*

*"Well, I went over there to drop off his medicine I had picked up from*

*Walgreens. My plan was to be in and out because I had shit to do, and I started feeling so uncomfortable around him, and the way he stares at me makes the hairs on the back of my neck stand up. You had so much going on. I didn't want to bother you. Plus, I thought I could handle things on my own. I walked into the bedroom to hand him the prescriptions. He grabbed me and threw me on the bed, where I land on my stomach, and he attacked me. I tried so hard to get up and get away, which really made him angry, and he started punching me in the back of the head until I blacked out. All while he raped me, I was going in and out of consciousness from the hits to the back of my head, or it could have been from the pain I feeling from the sexual attack. He kept repeatedly saying how he knew this pussy was going to be right, and 'I know my son ain't fucking you right, bitch.' Eventually, I was able to elbow him, get out his grasp, and get away. I jumped in my car and pulled off as he was coming out of the front door. I wasn't driving a whole minute before I felt my eyes getting heavy, and I blacked out."* I knew it was some shit she left out to protect my mental, but he straight violated. Fuck! What kind of husband was I if I couldn't protect my seeds and my wife?

"Damn, it's OK, ma. I'll take care of everything. Moe, quit blaming your-self for this shit because the accident wasn't your fault... I love you, baby." As I was about to console my wife a text message came through my burner, making it vibrate loudly on my desk. I looked at the message, and it was a text from Keys stating one of our traps was robbed, and one of our members that was named Shawn was headed my way. "Baby, I gotta head down to the ER. They have a GSW in route, and you know I have to be down there just in case I need to intervene somehow."

"Is it a KDB member?" she questioned with concern.

"Yeah!" I tapped her thigh so she could stand up, which she did. I gave her a hug and kissed her lips. "I'll see you later when I make it home. It might be late though." She nodded and then walked out of my office.

I couldn't even think clearly because I kept replaying the conversation over and over again. I had to put that shit in the back of my mind because I needed to go handle whatever the fallout would be from the shooting.

I grabbed my stethoscope and put it around my neck, my work

pager, and cell phone so I could head to the ER. I knew Damien or King would take care of the trap because they knew I was at work, and they knew I would hold things down at the hospital, considering I was an emergency-room physician.

Dr. Bennett Howard is what I went by when I was at work, but I also went by the alias Beast whenever I dealt with anything pertaining to KDB business. Only the lieutenants in our organization could put a face to the name Beast though, and I wanted to keep it that way for as long as I could. I did this for obvious reasons, but the main reason is so I could make moves in silence pertaining to KDB business.

As I walked through the ER, I stopped and asked the clerk to see if the new trauma patient had arrived. She let me know they hadn't, so I began walking around observing how things were flowing throughout the department. As I got ready to head toward pediatrics so I could check on Sam, I noticed an ambulance backing up to the ambulance bay entrance, positioning themselves so they could drop a patient off. They unloaded Shawn and headed my way with one of our lieutenants, Romello, following behind them. We made eye contact as I grabbed the end of the stretcher to help guide them to the trauma room he was assigned to. Mello knew not to make it public knowledge that we knew each other because under no circumstances am I to be affiliated with KDB at all. I just hoped the police didn't show up anytime soon snooping around, but that's why we try to keep our lieutenants away from public, gang-affiliated violence because once you get on the police radar, it was hard getting yourself off.

We wheeled the stretcher into the room, and things began moving at a very fast pace with Dr. Samuels being lead on the case. Being lead meant he ran the show so it wouldn't be straight chaos in the room.

"On the count of three, let's transfer the patient from the stretcher to the bed. One, two, three." Resident Samuels counted out loudly. "Can one of you guys give me a report on this case?" he asked, directing the question to one of the paramedics. I stood outside of the room with Diane and Romello, observing and listening to everything that was being said.

"This is nineteen-year-old Shawn Dawson, and we were called to transport him here because he was shot four times in the chest at close range. I believe all the bullets are within the chest cavity because I haven't found any exit wounds. From what I can tell, I think blood is collecting in his chest on the right because his lung sounds decreased on that side while en route here. I had given him two bags of fluids because his pulse and blood pressure was low, but it really didn't help increase either. He's been in and out of consciousness since we picked him up, and I had to put him on an oxygen mask because his oxygen level dropped to 85%. He received four milligrams of morphine five minutes ago, and I don't have a record of any allergies or past medical conditions. His brother rode with us in the ambulance, and he's currently standing in the hallway with Dr. Howard and Diane. Police should be here shortly and asked to make sure you save any bullet fragments retrieved from the patient please," the female paramedic blurted out in one breath.

They knew me and Diane well because we tried to be present for the traumas that came through the emergency room. I directed my attention toward Diane because I knew she was about to try and get information out of Romello, and I hoped he would follow protocol.

"Hello, sir. I'm Diane, and I'm the nurse manager in the ER. I just need to ask you a few questions that will help us better care for Mr. Dawson. Are you related to the patient?" Diane asked Rome with her hand extended so they could shake hands.

Initially, Mello looked at her hand like she had shit on it, but then he extended his hand and aggressively shook hers. "Yeah. This my little brother," Romello mumbled.

"OK, can you tell me your name and a phone number that we can use if we need to contact you regarding Mr. Dawson's care? We'll put you in his medical record as his emergency contact." I prayed he handled this shit correctly because Romello was fairly new to his lieutenant position, but he had been a member a little over two years.

"My name's Leo, and my cell phone just got turned off." Diane looked at his ass like he crazy because this nigga was standing there in Gucci from head to toe and some thousand-dollar Balenciaga tennis shoes. The other thing that was throwing me was that Romello was a lieutenant, and he shouldn't have been in the same vicinity of a gang-related shooting victim because we didn't want the cops questioning a KDB member if possible. That sent up a red flag for me because he should have given her up the dummy number we use that goes straight to Keys when dialed. Oh yeah, if this hasn't been mentioned before, Keys was the computer genius we had on the payroll. She was the first person we put on our payroll, and she was the highest paid employee we had because her expertise is the glue that held our business together.

"Leo, do you know of any allergies your brother may have or any medical conditions we should be aware of?" Diane questioned with a raised brow.

Mello hesitantly looked around before he dryly answered, "Nah".

Diane tried to gain trust with Mello trying to explain what was going on around us. "The doctors are going to check your brother out and then treat your brother's injuries. This is the time we ask the family to sit in the waiting area until he's stabilized. Once the doctors finish, they'll come out to the waiting area and give you an update. If you follow me, I can escort you to the waiting area." She walked toward the lobby, but Romello didn't move.

"Can you make sure someone comes out and update me with his condition? Our mother stays out of town, and I need to keep her updated until she can fly in," Mello questioned while looking me in my eyes. That let me know he needed to talk to me about whatever happened.

I spoke up so he would know that I would be out shortly to rap with him. "Hello, my name is Dr. Howard, and I'm the assistant director for this department. I'll personally come out and update you on your brother's condition." I introduced myself, letting him know I knew he needed to talk, and I would be out shortly when it was safe for us to talk. He turned in the opposite direction and followed Diane while the staff started treating Shawn.

When I walked back into Shawn's hospital room and looked at him, I realized how truly fucked up his condition was, and I couldn't believe he was still alive. Whoever shot him was trying to take his ass out. "Dr. Samuels, can you tell me your plan of care for Mr. Dawson?" I asked, already knowing how he was going to proceed, but I wanted it to at least look legit when I excused myself to update the family.

"Dr. Howard, for now, the plan is to place a chest tube, get a chest X-ray immediately following the tube placement, blood transfusion of two units, and he definitely needs to go to the operating room." I gave him a nod for my approval, and the staff continued working on him when suddenly the heart monitor alarms started going crazy. Shawn's heart stopped and went into a crazy rhythm, and with that particular rhythm, if it was not corrected immediately, it would cause his heart to give out. The nurse grabbed the resuscitation cart while one of the residents started chest compressions. I took this as my chance to go out and talk with Romello without being missed.

"Alright. I'm going to go let the family know what's going on." Dr. Samuels nodded his head, and I walked out to the waiting area in search for Mello. I spotted him all the way in the back of the waiting area room away from everyone. I signaled for him to follow me when he looked up, and we made eye contact. I led him into one of the private rooms we used to talk to families in. We walked in, and he closed the door behind him. He looked angry and frustrated as hell.

"So what's up? How this shit even happen?" I asked, giving him eye contact and my undivided attention. See, Dr. Howard's ass checked out, and I immediately went into Beast mode.

"So you know we been doing a trial run at the trap on Parkgate. Since it was only a trial, we only staffed the house with four niggas, which includes Shawn and Dre. So far, it seems like money and product have been moving well. Make a long story short, Shawn and Dre teamed up and stole some of the product.

"Today I go into the safe and pull the money and product out to do our daily inventory and money count, and off top, I could tell some shit wasn't right. They didn't touch the money because they know it gets counted every night, so we would have caught on sooner. I confronted Shawn, and his bitch ass starts talking reckless like I was a bitch-made nigga. I popped his ass four times in the chest right in front of Dre, and I honestly thought the nigga was dead. I step in the bathroom to call Wayne to let him know what happened and to see how he wanted me to handle things. As I walk back into the living room, I see this nigga Dre stuffing his cell phone into his pocket, but he was too slow because I caught him red-handed. Can you believe his rat ass called the police? I go crazy on that nigga and start pistol-whipping him. I would have killed him if Kurt didn't pull me off him. I drag Shawn down the street, call the police myself stating I heard shots, and when I went to see what happened, I found my brother laying on the ground bleeding. Kurt stays in the house with Dre until Wayne shows up, and I ride in the ambulance with Shawn, just to make sure this nigga didn't say shit to the paramedics or the po-po. I was praying I got a chance to end his life before we got here, but luck wasn't on my fuckin' side." He wiped his hand down his face and started pacing back and forth in front of me.

"That was some quick thinking on your part, so what did you do with Dre?" I asked with a tone of concern.

These two dumb asses thought they could get away with it because we were only doing a trial run at that location. They assumed we didn't have any cameras connected to the Hubb watching the activity in the house. They were correct because the cameras weren't connected to the Hubb's central computer system, but they were recording and were connected to a simple app that could be accessed from our cell phones. That was the problem with the trials—it was a double-edged sword. Yes, it told us what potential profit we could make, but it also allowed the product and money to be accessible to all the workers.

"Wayne came and shut down the trap. He took Dre, the drugs, and money back to the Hubb," he offered.

"Mell, my nigga… you really are losing your touch, my mans," I said while patting his shoulder and then back. "Considering you're one of our best hittas, it was surprising to me you didn't hit him between the eyes… That has me thinking if there something I should know now about what happened because I'm going to be pissed if some shit come out later regarding this situation." I could see the wheels in his head turning, and you could tell he had a devil on one shoulder and an angel on the other one.

"Yeah... I hesitated before I shot him. Right before I pulled the trigger, he started begging for his life and told me he had a son on the way. Bennie, I had a lapse in judgment for a second and sympathized with this idiot. It was only because I wouldn't want someone taking me out before I could even meet my seed. But the more I thought about it, I realized they didn't give a fuck about me or the consequences that would come from his stealing. Y'all would kill all our asses if it came out somebody was stealing, and it looked suspicious, and that shit pissed me off, so I made Shawn get on his knees, I closed my eyes for a second, and let my hammer rip. I didn't realize he tried to jump up to prevent from being shot in the head, so his chest took the hits." He lowered his head because I could tell he felt like shit because Shawn made him look like a soft ass fool. He turned toward the wall and punched it, and that made me furious.

"Nigga, I know you're upset, but don't be blowing up the spot I work at. I don't need these muthafuckas calling security and asking me questions. Be mad at your muthafuckin' self because you fucked up. The only reason you ain't lying in a bed next to ya boy Shawn is because you're Damien's cousin!" I yelled at his bitch ass. "I should make you take your ass back there to clean your own mess up, but I can't afford for you to do some more sloppy shit."

The longer I was confined in this small room with Romello, the more pissed off I got. I grabbed the doorknob to leave, but instead of walking out, I turned back around and rocked the fuck out of him with a nice two piece. He fell back on his ass, and I stood over him, chest heaving up and down, and gave him fair warning. "We're not allowed to make mistakes in this game, muthafucka. Mistakes can get us all killed. We... do... not... have sympathy for our fucking enemies, period. If this job is too much for you to handle, let us know so we can replace you. I'm pretty sure someone would be more than happy to take your place." I didn't even wait for a response. I just walked out the room and headed to the back so I could fix his damn mess.

I walked into Shawn's room where his nurse was, and luckily, she was the only person in there still providing care. He was still alive but barely, and that was only gonna be the truth for another maybe ten minutes max. "Excuse me, Theresa, did radiology come and do his chest X-ray yet?" I questioned. She never turned to look at me because she was so focused on what she was doing, but she told me no. "Well, can you go call them and ask them how long it'll be before they get here? I think the surgeons are on their way down for him." You would have thought I asked this bitch to fix world hunger or something. She rolled her eyes, smacked her lips, and stormed out of the room, and that's why I couldn't stand that bitch.

I only had five minutes max to get the job done. I grabbed three syringes of potassium chloride out of the crash cart, pushed them through the higher port on the IV tubing, dropped the syringes in my pocket, and walked out of the room like nothing happened. *I'll discard the syringes in a sharps container in another department,* I thought to myself.

See, when potassium chloride is given in a high enough dose, it stopped the heart, and I put it in a higher port so when the medicine reached Shawn's bloodstream, I would already be outside of the room looking busy.

I walked out of the room and over to Diane to make small talk until all hell broke loose, which should have taken only a couple of minutes. Five minutes later, alarms started going crazy because Shawn's heart stopped beating, and the staff ran into his room in an attempt to save his life again. I stood there and waited for the doctor to call time of death so I could leave.

I felt my cell phone vibrating in my pocket. I pulled it out and answered it because it was Damien. "Hey, what's up?" I questioned while looking around. He told me about everything going on with KJ and that they were about to leave the hospital and head toward the Hubb. "Alright, I'm leaving the hospital also, so I'll meet y'all there." He asked me did I handle Shawn. "Yeah, that's handled. I'll talk y'all when I get there." I hung up the phone and stared at the team in Shawn's room trying to get his heart started back up. I wished they would just call time of death because I was ready to go, and they were pissing me off because they were working too fucking hard to save his rat ass life.

"Time of death, 1435," Dr. Samuels yells. *Finally,* I thought as I walked out of the emergency department to go handle other business that needed my attention.

# 5

# OLD HABITS DIE HARD

## MR. DAMIEN WASHINGTON

### "Damien"

MY UPBRINGING HAD BEEN like the worst hood Lifetime movie you could think of. I had amazing parents that did any and everything for me, and they made sure I didn't need or want for shit. We lived in a suburb called Cleveland Heights up until they died. Both of my parents worked outside the home, but I really never could remember exactly what type of work they did. They worked hard, and we ended up moving out of the hood when I was really young but not without developing a lot of haters, which included my aunt. She couldn't stand my mother because she said she thought she was better than everybody, but that was far from the truth.

I was ten years old when my parents died, and that was the worse day of my life. My mother drove her and my dad headfirst into a semi truck, and they died instantly. She had been battling postpartum depression after having my baby sister. My mother was OK until my baby sister died from SIDS when she was one month old. Her depression went from bad to worse, and after she dropped me off over my aunt's one day, and that was the last day I saw my parents alive.

My aunt took custody of me so I wouldn't go into the foster care system. Initially, when I moved with my aunt, things were really good. Romello and I always got along very well, so when I moved in, we became closer and looked at each other more like brothers instead of cousins. We were a tight family until my aunt started dating her loser ass nigga. I was about fifteen or sixteen when they first started kickin' it, and two months later, she moved this nigga in.

From the beginning, that nigga hated me and Mello's guts, and we couldn't figure out why. He never could hold a job, never contributed toward household shit, stole money from my aunt, and constantly cheated on her. When he started being physically abusive toward her, Mello and I beat that nigga's ass bad as fuck. She was mad at us for a long time after that, but I didn't give a fuck. She even threatened to put us out if we didn't show his triflin" ass some respect. She had me fucked up because respect with me is earned and not given. The day Romello and I turned eighteen, she put us out because her nigga told her to. I swear I wanted to peel that nigga's scalp back, but she chose that nigga over her own blood. Thank God I was dating Camille, and her aunt allowed me to move in with them when she found out I was homeless.

I met my beautiful, chocolate wife while we both were attending Glenville High School. Ever since the first time I saw her standing around with her girls after school, I knew I had to have her. After we had sex the first time, I knew I was going to make her my wife and the mother of my children. See, back in the day, most girls that lived in our neighborhood was run through and friendly with the pussy, but not Camille. The first time we had sex, she was a virgin, which I admired because she was probably the only virgin I ever fucked. Niggas were hatin' like a muthafucka when I cuffed her ass because she was wifey material, and they knew it. Plus, she had book smarts, street smarts, and a bad ass body. That's why the girls hated her, and the niggas wanted her.

We had two beautiful daughters: Alexandra, who we call Alex, and the youngest is Danielle, but we call her Dani. We decided to get married because we refused to bring another child into this world out of wedlock, so we got married shortly after finding out she was pregnant with Dani.

I can admit, over the years, I had problems with monogamy. I got caught cheating a lot, but every time Camille found out, she would be mad for a bit, but she always forgave me. The last time I cheated, it was with this broad named Chanel. Chanel and I had been off and on for years, but the last time, Camille threatened to divorce me if she ever found out I cheated again. She was so upset, she lost total control and almost killed me and Chanel, and it scared Camille because she didn't know she was capable of even taking things as far as she did. So ever since, I had been on the straight and narrow, but old habits die hard.

"Ring, ring, ring. Call from the King." My phone ringed through the Bluetooth of my car speakers and scared the holy hell out of me, pulling me out of my thoughts.

"Answer."

"Hey, nigga. Are you on your way to scoop me from the hospital before I choke the life out of Tammy retarded ass?" I couldn't do shit but laugh because I think he hated his wife just as much as we all did. The only reason he hadn't divorced her ass was that she was KJ's mother, and he felt like he owed her some type of loyalty because she helped him recover from injuries he received while serving the country. I told that nigga many times, he had paid her back tenfold since then. I couldn't wait until he realized he didn't owe her ass shit, and I was hoping it didn't take long before he came to his senses. Since Sam was back, maybe he would get some motivation to terminate her ass.

I know you're wondering why I dislike her so much. First, it's because she's a bonafide hoe! The night she slept with King, she knew what she was doing, and we all believe she got pregnant on purpose. The other reason is that the tramp blackmailing me.

Someone brought it to my attention Tammy was cheating on King with one of our workers. That in itself shows how nasty and disrespectful the bitch is. How you gonna fuck the homie, and then to make matters worse, she fucks down the food chain? She threatened to tell Camille about me and Chanel fucking around again and about us sharing a two-year-old son together. Tammy thought she was doing something by telling me that, but all she did was get her friend fucked up. The same night she threatened me is the same night I choked Chanel out while I was tearing her guts up.

When she came to, I was getting dressed and walked out without saying a fuckin' word, so yes, I punished her and the pussy that night. I specifically told Chanel ass not to say shit to Tammy about us fucking around again, but she didn't listen, and she suffered the consequences for talking too much. I also told her to quit fucking with Tammy, and if she didn't, I told her I wouldn't fuck with her again. I knew I would find out if she didn't listen, so I was trying my best to figure out a way to keep my wife from filing for divorce when she found out the truth about me and Chanel.

King yelled through the phone, "Damn, nigga, did you hear me calling your fucking name?" Shit, I forgot I was on the phone with his ass. Life got my ass stressed the fuck out right now.

"Nigga, yeah. I'm trying to find a parking spot now. Your bitch ass needs to quit crying so much. Didn't nobody tell you to have a baby and marry Tammy slow ass. That fuck up is all yours to own, my nigga. I don't see how you deal with it personally, but I guess to each his own. I just parked, so it'll take me about fifteen minutes to walk up there, and I ain't staying long. I love my nephew, but I can't breathe the same air as your wife for too long. Bye!" I hung up and got started on the forty-mile walk up to the ICU. KJ had been in the ICU since he had surgery two days before, and the last time King updated me, KJ's condition was the same. I figured that was better than it getting worse, but dealing with KJ's condition had been hard on him. Shit, all I could do was help pick up his slack as much as possible so he could focus on KJ as much as he could.

I finally made it to his room and tried to brace myself for seeing my lil' dude fucked up like that. Before I could get in the room good, Tammy looked my way and mugged the fuck out of me, and you know I returned the gesture.

"What's up, King? What are the doctors saying?" King stood, gave me dap, and pulled me into a brotherly hug.

"The doctor just left right before you walked in. He said that he thinks the infection might have caused some irreversible damage to his organs, primarily his kidneys. They've started him on a medicine to try and protect whatever functions he has left, but they doubt if the kidney's condition will get better. He said eventually KJ will have to go on dialysis or get a kidney transplant when his stops working altogether." King crossed his arms across his chest and started pacing in front of KJ's bed before finishing. "Other than that, everything else is still the same."

"He's going to pull through this shit, man, so don't stress. Also, you know we're all going to get tested to see if we can give him one of our kidneys, and if we're not matches, we'll do what we have to find him one." I genuinely vocalized.

Tammy's *pessimistic* ass grunted and then started talking garbage, as usual. Just in case I didn't say this before, I hated that bitch! "Y'all niggas kill me acting like y'all got all this fucking pull like y'all the mob or some shit. Y'all niggas ain't shit, ain't never been shit, and ain't never gonna be shit. Yeah, y'all doin a little something in these streets, but y'all ain't that fucking important. What the fuck you need to do is worry about that bitch bringing her ass in my son's room again, because the next time, I'm beating that hoe's ass." I assumed she was talking about Sam, but you never knew with her. I refused to argue in front of my nephew because he had enough going on. I was going to keep my mouth closed and just leave so King and I could get to this business meeting we had setup.

When King stopped pacing and turned to look Tammy's way with the look of death, I knew wasn't shit good going to come from that. "Aw shit," I whispered under my breath.

"I'm going to say this one time and one time only. That woman ain't did shit but save our son's life, and your disrespectful ass wants to threaten her because she's trying to support my son while he recovers. What's so fucked up is the only reason you've been here around the clock is because you're scared she's going to come back. You triflin' as fuck. Keep acting a fool up here, and I'm going to ban your ass from seeing my seed, and I dare for you to try me," King said with venom dripping from his voice.

I was so glad she didn't say shit else. King walked out of the room, and I followed. As we walked down the hall, he ran into KJ's fine ass nurse and told her to call his cell phone if something changed or if she needed to talk to him for some reason.

Once we made it to the car, I sat down, grabbed a blunt out of the ashtray, and handed it to him. Normally. he didn't indulge much, but if he does, he waited until after business was handled for the day and he's at home chilling. But this nigga needed to hit something before he burst a blood vessel in his brain.

He lit the blunt, took two long pulls, and passed it to me. "This some nice ass kush. Is this the shit Bennie been working on? Man, I love my son to death, but I swear I wish I didn't have to deal with her for another ten years."

"What the fuck happened, now?" I asked.

"Tammy just gets on my fuckin' nerves all the time, doing ghetto as shit. Like the shit she did to Sam yesterday when she came by KJ's room to see how he was doing. Time Sam walked into the room, Tammy started acting a complete ass. Tammy told Sam she had to leave and as Sam and I ignored her dumb ass and kept talking, Tammy called the nurse and asked the nurse to call security, and told them Sam wasn't allowed to visit KJ again. Nigga, that shit was embarrassing as hell. Sam handled that shit like a G though. She said, 'OK' and walked out. Tammy wanted to argue and fight, but Sam too classy for that shit. Plus, this is her place of business," King said, grinning big and shit.

"Baby sis would have mopped the floor with Tammy's ass! I would pay a million dollars to be a fly on the fucking wall when she beats that ass because you know that shit coming, and it's going to be comical. Especially if y'all start fuckin' around again." We both started laughing hard as fuck because we both knew the ass whoopin' was coming, and that was inevitable, especially since Tammy wanted to turn up on Sam. Whenever it did happen, I doubt if Tammy even get a lick in. The question wasn't if it was going to happen, but the question was when it was going to happen at that point.

"So is that why I had to show my ID to come up and see him?" I questioned.

"Yeah." King looked down at his phone because that shit kept ringing. "Every time I leave, this crazy bitch calls me a million fucking times for no reason but to get on my nerves," King said, and then he blocked her ass. He only did that because we were about to go handle business, and we couldn't be focused on other shit while doing it. We had a meeting with the commissioner and mayor of Cleveland, Frank Jackson. Over the next two weeks, we had so many meetings setup with people we had on payroll to catch them up on the plans we were initiating next month.

We were laying out our plans, the role each person would play in phase two of our plans, and we gave them an incentive to fall in line. I didn't foresee any resistance, so I was very optimistic the transition would be smooth.

I started my car and headed toward downtown because we had less than forty-five minutes to make it there and setup before the mayor and his team arrived for the meeting.

"Ring, ring, ring. Call from, King's Bitch." I looked at the screen, and King laughed hard as hell when my Bluetooth announced the name I have Tammy saved as. My fuckin' Bluetooth had no chill. The only reason this bitch Tammy dialed my line was because King blocked her. I wasn't King. I planned on cussin' the bitch straight out.

"King, this bitch out of line calling my fucking phone. I'm going to have Camille tag that ass again if she keeps playing with me." I was about to decline the shit, but I fucked around and hit the answer button on my steering wheel.

"Damien!" Tammy screamed through the phone, catching me off guard.

"Bitch, quit fucking—"

I couldn't even finish my sentence because she cut me off yelling again.

"KJ's dead! He's dead!" is all we heard before the line went dead.

# 6

# MISERY LOVES COMPANY

## MRS. CAMILLE WASHINGTON

### "Camille"

THE LAST FEW weeks since KJ died had been hard on us all. I had even humbled myself to try and be there for Tammy while she grieved because King wasn't fucking with her period. Even with everything on my plate, I still found time to call her every couple of days just to make sure she was still with the living. I could tell that the grief she was going through was changing her, possibly for the good, but it could have been a front. I had so much empathy for her and King because I wouldn't have been sane if I had to bury my child. Damien probably would have had to have my ass committed into the psych ward at St. Vincent.

I decided to call Tammy and check on her, and when I did, she asked me if I would meet her for lunch at Wasabi Japanese Steakhouse in Beachwood, Ohio. I couldn't remember the last time I had gone out to eat, so I jumped on her offer quickly.

Once I arrived, I noticed she was already there and had already been seated. As I approached the table, she stood and pulled me into a hug once I was within an arm's reach of her. When she noticed my reluctance, she released the embrace and sat back down in her chair. I could tell she was embarrassed, but I couldn't do shit but be real because I didn't do phony. I wasn't going to sit there and act like we're best friends, because we weren't.

We took our seats, and I began looking over my menu. I don't know why because I eat the same thing whenever I go there. Once we placed our food orders, I took in Tammy's appearance, and you could tell the struggle was real, and KJ's death was really affecting her. Normally, Tammy's hair was done, makeup was flawless, and she didn't wear anything unless it had a label. So the lady that was sitting in front of me felt foreign. She didn't have on any makeup, her hair was pulled up into a messy bun, and she had on jeans and a simple T-shirt. A far cry from what I was used to.

"So what's up? Why did you ask me to meet you here? Don't take that as me being mean, because I'm not, but I'm just getting straight to the point," I asked, trying to read her body language, but the only era I was getting from her is fear.

She cleared her throat and took a brief pause. I could tell she was trying to choose her words wisely. "Well, I asked you here because ever since my son died, everyone who I considered to be my friend or family has turned their back on me. Other than the guy I've been seeing, you're the only other person that's shown me any compassion, and I know that was hard, considering how you feel about me." Our waitress walked up to our table, and Tammy stopped talking. Once she walked away, she continued talking. "Being honest, I wasn't going to ever tell you this because my loyalty lies with Chanel. Well, it did, but she turned her back on me when I needed her the most, thanks to your husband. She's not a real friend though because real friends don't leave you hanging like that. Damien and Chanel started back sleeping together about a year ago."

"Wait, what the fuck are you talking about, Tammy? He ain't fucking with that bitch again. He wouldn't do that bullshit to me… He wouldn't do that shit to me, Tammy." I could slowly but surely feel myself losing control at that point. I stood up quickly, placing both of my palms on the table, knocking my chair over in the process scaring the hell out of some patrons and Tammy. I knew it may not seem like it, but I was really trying to calm myself down. I had to get some type of control of the emotions I was feeling. I bowed my head, closed eyes, and took some deep breaths and started praying to God silently to calm me down.

"Look, I'm sorry you have to find out this way, but I just feel they're doing you dirty... It's more, Camille... it's more." When I looked up and made eye contact with her, I realized she had tears rolling down her face. I gave her a confused look because I didn't understand why she was so upset. Shit, I was the one being cheated on, not her, but what could be worse than him cheating on me?

"Shit!" I mumbled under my breath shaking my head side to side because I was praying she wasn't about to say what I was thinking. "No, no, no," I cried out.

Before she could even tell me the rest, sobs left my throat, and I broke down in an uncontrollable cry. "I'm so sorry—"

I cut her off. I just needed her to tell me, because if she said what I think she was insinuating, I was killing him and her.

"Just tell me!" I yelled, slamming my hand down on the table again, making food go everywhere. Tammy jumped out of her skin with her scary ass. She should be scared, because at that point, anybody could catch a fade. Hell, I had beaten the fuck out of her before. No... let me rephrase that. I damn near killed her ass one day. Her smart ass was being too disrespectful.

"The father of Chanel's son DJ is Damien." I gasped at the words that left her mouth.

My knees buckled, and I fell backward and landed in my seat that the waitress had just stood up moments before. Tammy walked around the table, trying to hug me around the neck, but that was the wrong move... I punched her dead in her nose. She immediately grabbed at her nose, and blood started gushing out of it.

"You broke my nose, bitch!" Chanel yelled.

She was lucky I was so focused on killing my husband and that bitch Chanel, because otherwise, I would have been digging off in her ass for calling me a bitch. Instead, I ran out of the restaurant, jumped in my car, and pulled off crazily. The tears began clouding my vision as I drove home, crying uncontrollably and upset. I pulled into my driveway, put my car in park, and just broke down completely.

"No, No, No!" I screamed out while slamming my fist numerous times on my steering wheel.

I sat in the car for about thirty minutes before I was able to muster up enough strength to walk into the house. Thank God the kids were still at summer camp because I needed a little peace and quiet to think about what I wanted to do next. I laid across the couch in the fetal position, crying my eyes out, eventually falling asleep. Banging on my front door tore me out of my sleep, scaring the hell out of me. *Bitch!*

"Wait, I'm coming!" I yelled as I angrily pulled the door open and saw Moe standing there raising two bottles of wine, and Sam raised a bag of Popeyes chicken, and my stance immediately softened. I left them standing there and walked back into the family room and laid back on the couch. I totally forgot we planned on having a sleepover and for the nannies to take the kids to Great Wolf Lodge for the weekend.

Sam angrily asked, "What the fuck did Damien do this time, boo?" I couldn't even answer her because if I said the words, it would have made the shit real. Sam realized something wrong, and she pulled me into her arms, and started rocking us back and forth while rubbing my back in small circles. "Moe, come here please and bring the wine and some glasses.

"OK, here I come!" she yelled from the kitchen.

I finally calmed down enough to try and tell them what was going on. I didn't even know how to start the conversation off and to tell these two what the piece of shit had done.

"Does this have something to do with you meeting up with Tammy? Best friend, you're starting to really scare me. Please tell me what's going on. Is it the kids? Please tell me what's going on!" Sam begged.

I grabbed some Kleenex off the coffee table and blew my nose and cleaned my face up as much as possible, stalling for time. "Tammy asked me to lunch to tell me Damien's fucking around with Chanel againnnnnnn!" I cried out. "An-And her son's father is *Dame!*"

"*Nooo*, Camille. He wouldn't do no low-down shit like that." Moe challenged with wide eyes.

"Bitch, what the fuck I look like lying about some shit like this?" I stood and started pacing and praying over and over again. I needed God to calm me down before I did some shit to land me in county jail, real talk. When I thought back over all the years I had been with Damien, I got mad at myself because I had given my all to that man. At times, I loved him more than I loved myself, and he had me out there looking like a goddamn fool!

"I've been riding with this nigga since I was fourteen years old, and the only thing I've asked of him in return is his loyalty." I walked over to the bookshelf and grabbed the canister from the top shelf that Damien kept his weed stash in, praying he had a blunt already rolled. *Thank God*, I thought to myself when I looked inside, and it was three fat ones looking back at me. I grabbed the lighter and fired one up and took a nice pull. I coughed a couple of times because it was strong as hell. I passed it over to Moe and grabbed my glass of wine taking half of it to the dome.

"Mill, do you think it's smart just to believe what she's saying? You know they say, misery loves company, and she doesn't like any of us, so how you know she's not lying to fuck up your home because hers so fucked up? I think you should talk to Damien first before making any rash decisions," Sam angrily spat. What Sam was saying could have been true, but I knew in my heart she wasn't lying. Sam hated Tammy, and she would never admit it, but she was jealous of Tammy because she was able to marry and give a child to the love of Sam's life, *King*.

"That girl ain't lying. I knew something had been off with him for the last couple of months. I chalked it up to the hustle and bustle of the game, but I knew something was off… I just didn't think he would cheat again, especially after the shit that happened the last time." I grabbed my cell phone and pulled up a picture I had on my phone from KJ's last birthday party, where all the kids posed for a picture. I threw my phone over to Sam on the couch, and she caught it. "Look at that shit, and you tell me if you think that's my husband's ugly ass son.

I ain't never paid attention to his Ninja Turtle-looking ass before, but they're damn near twins."

They both looked at the picture on my phone. Sam and Moe simultaneously said, "Wow!" They both placed a hand over their mouth in shock after looking at the picture.

After a few minutes of silence, Moe burst out laughing loud and hard as hell. She was bent over and everything with tears coming out of her eyes. "Bitch, how you gonna talk about the little boy like that? How you gonna call him a Ninja Turtle?" Her laughter became so contagious, Sam and I started laughing too. The laughter helped. It calmed me down some, because about five minutes before, I was in the mood to take the thirty-minute drive to Chanel's house and put a bullet in her head.

"Why would he do this to us, *again*? Why?" I questioned, knowing that was an answer they couldn't give me. Sam stood, shrugged her shoulders, and walked into the kitchen, returning with another bottle of wine, topping off our wine glasses. She plopped down on the couch next to me and exhaled a breath before speaking.

"You're about to be mad because I'm about to spit some true shit to you, boo, but just know this is coming from a place of love. The reason he cheats is that you've allowed him to get away with doing the shit to you for years. Don't get me wrong, Damien's a good man and father, but he's a terrible ass husband. When he cheated the first time, you took him back, and that was fine because everyone makes mistakes, but bitch, time after time you have taken him back. In his mind, he feels he can cheat, and when he gets caught, he knows all he has to do is finesse your ass, and you take him back with open arms. And if we're keepin' it one hundred, the only reason you're this mad and possibly questioning divorce is because it's possible Damien's the child's father." I couldn't stand that bitch, but I couldn't do shit but respect what she said, because Sam just read my ass!

"You're speaking all facts," I acknowledged the part I played in it. The truth was Damien's not capable of being faithful to me, and for them to have a child means he's out here raw doggin' the hoe, putting my life in jeopardy. AIDS/HIV was real out there. "Y'all, I don't think I can do this anymore. I think I'm done this time. I deserve more, and I don't think he's capable of giving it to me."

I couldn't sit there anymore talking about my fucked-up life. I was getting sleepy, and I needed to be alone and think. "I'm going to bed. I'll see y'all in the morning." I didn't even wait for a response before heading up the steps. I closed my eyes in an attempt of trying to go to sleep, but all the memories of past events and our possible future started invading my mind, torturing the hell out me.

I grabbed my phone and started typing because I needed to express how I was feeling to my dear old husband. It wasn't fair I was going through that hurt alone, considering he was the cause of the pain I was feeling. I knew he didn't have his personal cell phone on, but by the time that bitch turned it on, he would get a piece of my ass to kiss.

Normally, when they are out of town, they leave their cell phones off until they touch back down in Cleveland. But I needed to get that shit off my chest right then, and he needed to know how hurt I was. I picked up my phone and began typing. It took me thirty minutes to type the entire message. I kept erasing and rewriting parts. *Fuck it*, I thought and hit send, cut my phone off, closed my eyes, and I tried my best to go to sleep.

**Me:** *Hubbie, I didn't want to do this like this, but I'm drunk and pissed, so it is what it is. I never thought you could find a way to hurt me worse than you have in the past, but I give you a standing ovation because you did it. I know you back fucking with Chanel, and please don't deny it. I knew something's been off for a while, but I didn't have the courage to look for shit because I knew the hurt would be too much. I made myself very clear the last time you cheated that we were over if it happened again. I almost went to jail behind that hoe Chanel and your community-dick having ass. If you're going to cheat, it could at least be a bitch on my level or higher, but nooooo, your weak ass downgrades. You go snag the same gutter rat that has been trying to break our marriage up for years. You, Bennie, and King begged me to take your black ass back the last time, and I did because of the love I had for my brothers and our family. I didn't want to split our family up, but you can thank yourself for that. I'm done with your ass and this discussion. I have to* *live with the part I've played in this, but I learn from my mistakes. The next nigga will treat me how I'm supposed to be treated. I hope it was worth it, Damien, because you've lost your family, and I'm filing for divorce. Don't bring your ass back to my house. All intruders will be shot, bitch!*

*P.S. Oh, yeah. Tell that bitch it's on sight! -Wifey*

# 7

# SAFE IN HIS ARMS

## "SAM"

As Moe and I sat there silently watching Camille walk upstairs, my heart broke for my sister. It made me think about my situation because they're so similar. The only difference between the two is Damien would never give Mill a divorce willingly, and Brian is the one who decided to file for our divorce. When he filed, yes, we were both unhappy, but never in a million years did I think we would actually sign on the dotted line. I was thinking maybe we should try seeing a counselor first or do some type of couple's retreat, but as time passed, I knew it was deeper than us both not being happy, and boy was I right.

As time passed, it became mistakenly obvious my husband was cheating on me, and whomever the bitch was, was deep in his head, and he probably felt he was in love with her. That's why I hired a private investigator right before I moved back to Cleveland to help shed some light on what the fuck was really going on. The PI found out that Brian had been cheating on me about three years with multiple women, but this last chick, he had been fucking her for a year and a half, and she was a surgical technician he worked with. She was supposedly five months pregnant, and he proposed to her right before he asked me for a divorce. My PI told me he thought Brian was pushing for a rapid divorce because he wanted to marry Alanna before she had their baby. Niggas ain't shit.

Moe pulled me out of my thoughts by asking, "Do you think she's going to really divorce Dame this time?"

"Moe, your guess is as good as mine. I do believe this may be the straw though because of the little boy, DJ. It's one thing to cheat, but to create a life from your infidelities is fucked up. Damien may be an ass, but he's a good father, so he's going to want his child to be around his siblings. I don't think Camille can handle his indiscretions thrown in her face every time the child's around. And knowing my friend, Camille's petty ass not going to accept the little boy either. You know I'm going through something similar, and I know for a fact a bitch like me could never forgive any shit like that.

"Plus, anyone who knows Camille knows how bad she wanted to give Damien a son to carry on his legacy, but her body wouldn't allow it, but here come this popcorn hoe giving him what she couldn't. N-O-P-E." I spelled out. "Camille ain't getting over this one!" I said with confidence. I grabbed the wine bottle and topped off Moe's wine glass and poured a little in mine.

"Yeah, that's a hard pill to swallow. I don't think I could move on from that either when you break it down like that. Do you think we should call Bennie and King and give them a heads up about everything?" Moe questioned.

"No… I think we should just wait until we talk to Camille and see how she wants to handle things in the morning. She's not out looking for him or Chanel to kill them right now since he's out of town, so he's not in immediate danger. Now when his plane touches down in two days, everybody needs to be on high alert because she might really kill him this time. I swear I want to fuck Damien up myself right now." I answered in a frustrated tone.

Moe questioned with a raised eyebrow, "Sam, is the bitch pussy that good, made of gold, or maybe her throat's lined with silk? Somebody tell me something, because I don't understand it at all. How can a man jeopardize his home like that? I wonder if we're not seeing the bigger picture here? Do you think he has feelings for Chanel?"

"I have no idea, but I know he done fucked up, and there's possibly no coming back from it. I just feel sorry for the kids because they're the innocent ones, but they suffer the most. They don't know a world where they have to split their time between their mom and dad's house. All I can do is pray for everyone because it seems like the devil been *really* busy around here!" I pushed out a breath in frustration. "I'm just tired of our family being attacked. When will it all stop? *Damn!*" We sat there in silence for about five minutes, and I was thinking about everything that had happened since I had been back, and I was questioning whether I made the right decision by moving back.

I heard sniffles coming from Moe. When I looked up, she had tears running down her face, looking extremely upset for some reason. I knew the stuff going on with Camille didn't have her that upset, so I was trying to figure what was going on.

"Sam, I can't hold this shit in anymore. It's truly eating me alive." I moved over to the couch she was sitting on and wrapped her in my arms.

"Moe, you can tell me anything, babe, without judgment. I love you, and I'm here to help you through whatever. So what's up?"

"I'm so tired of fucking crying." She screeched out loud. "This is so hard to talk about, but it's time. I've been holding this shit in for over two years, and it's been eating me up like a disease. I just told Bennie, and I'm so scared for him right now. He's been so distant that in a way I wish I hadn't said anything. You remember the day I had the accident, right?" I nodded but didn't open my mouth because I didn't want to interrupt her. "The accident happened when I was trying to get away from Maxwell after he beat me... and raped me. During the attack, I was hit in the head multiple times, causing me to have a concussion. That's why I passed out when I was trying to get away from him and had the car accident." She bowed her head and completely broke down, but I couldn't say anything or comfort her because I was frozen in place from shock. How could someone be so fucking evil?

Finally, I was able to snap out of it and say a few words to possibly comfort her. "Oh, Moe, I'm so sorry... It's going to be OK. Over time, y'all will be able to move past this." I didn't know what else to say. I felt like how much more pain did this man have to cause us before it was enough.

"Sam, I don't think Bennie wants me anymore. Ever since I told him, he's been treating me different. He won't talk to me, and he's been avoiding me like the plague. I thought after I told him what happened, things would get better between us, but it's made things worse. Sam, I can't handle losing him too." She looked at me with sadness and fear all throughout her eyes. She loved the fuck out of my brother, and I could tell she was scared of what may come from that revelation. She knew Bennie was going to kill our father, and I could tell she was concerned about how it was going to affect him mentally. Especially since how he acted after our mother's death.

"Moe, you're not going to lose him. My brother loves you too much to push you out of his life. He's just upset and trying to work through this shit the best way he can. Think about it like this, he feels he failed all the women in his life. In his mind, he feels he couldn't protect me or our mom from that monster. Now, he's being told he couldn't protect his own family either. That would be a hard pill for any man to swallow. Give him the space he needs to figure out the best way for him to handle the situation, that's it. In due time, he'll come to you so both of you can support each other through this. I promise. I know my brother like the back of my hand. Come and give me a hug and go upstairs and call him and talk to your husband. He may be more open to talking about things since you're on the phone and not actually in his face."

She responded, "OK," and headed upstairs to call him, leaving me downstairs by myself. I didn't want to tell her that he had already told me what happened, and he expressed how he felt about the entire situation, so I had to play it off like I didn't know anything.

It weighed heavy on my heart though that my father did that to her. Ever since Bennie told me about Moe, I had been having nightmares of the stuff I went through at the hands of *our father*. I thought the shit I went through growing up was behind me, but it wasn't, and that situation let me know I still had work to do to get over the trauma caused by my upbringing.

I felt like I was going down memory lane because the memories were flooding my mind, and I began to feel like that sixteen-year-old getting beat with a belt just because. All the times he smacked the shit out of me, choked me out, and kicked and stomped me until I passed out were giving me great anxiety at that moment. That man made my life a living hell, and I was glad he was going through a hell of his own fighting sclerosis of the liver—a battle he was losing terribly.

I stood up and started pacing the floor trying to calm myself down and do as my therapist showed me many times before. She would walk me through an exercise to decrease my anxiety and hopefully relax my thoughts at the same time. So I closed my eyes and went to a time where I felt safe from harm and at peace. The tears started to roll down my face, and I didn't even try to wipe them. I laid down on the couch, thinking about the last time I *really* felt safe, and even though I was crying, those were happy tears. A smile crossed my face when I went back to the night of Bennie's birthday party.

*Saturday, July 30, 2011*

*As I slid my body into the dress I picked out for Bennie's party, I smiled in awe of how amazing I looked in this dress. I decided to go outside of my conservative norm and wear a spaghetti-strapped, gold-sequined dress that stopped about two inches from my knees and had a high split on the right thigh, taking panties out of the equation. The dress was slightly loose and had a deep V in the back that stopped right above my ass. On my feet, I wore a pair of five-inch, gold Giuseppe Zanotti sandals with wing tips on the back. I had my hair pulled up into a tight and clean ponytail, with thirty inches of hair draping over my right breast. My makeup was flawless, and my makeup artist decided to use a pair of real gold-accented eyelashes and a gold lipstick from the Keyshia Ka'oir Glitzstick line.*

*My nerves really started to get the best of me when my driver pulled up to the B-Stone where Bennie was having his party. I checked my makeup, hair, and clothes before I exited the truck. When I made it to the VIP area, I* noticed some KDB members I knew, but I really never interacted with them much, so I didn't know but maybe three or four people, and they were in the process of getting white boy wasted. I looked around trying to spot King, but he was nowhere in sight. A waitress walked up and handed me champagne flute filled with Moet. I took it straight to the dome and stuck my glass out so she could pour me some more. I walked over to where everyone was sitting and said hello to everyone. Then one of my favorite songs came on; Rihanna's "Bitch Better Have My Money" started blaring through the speakers, and immediately, my hips began swaying, winding, and started twerking.

I grabbed a fine ass nigga that was standing maybe ten feet away eyeing me up and down and pulled him to the dance floor. I began winding my hips and started grinding my ass on his dick. By the middle of the song, I looked up and saw King walk through the door, but I didn't think he spotted me yet, and honestly, he probably wasn't even looking for me considering this was one of the only things I had really come to. Ying Yang Twins' "Salt Shaker" came on, and I immediately looked around for Camille. My bitch was always right on time. She got in front of me, and we started twerking, tearing the dance floor up together. Moe came out and joined us, and we were in our girl's zone, grinding and winding our hips and rapping all the words to the song. Halfway through the song, Bennie crept up behind Moe, and Damien did the same with Camille. I continued dancing solo without a care in the world because this the most fun I had in so long.

Suddenly, I felt someone's arms come around my waist from the back, and he was grinding his thick rod on my ass. I tried to turn around to see who it is, but he wouldn't release my waist enough so I could. He wanted to play. Two could play that game. The DJ put on Mystikal's "Shake It Fast", and I lost it. I started grinding faster and harder, touching my toes, and when I came back up, I felt him brush his lips against the back of my neck, sending a shock down my entire spine and making the hairs on my arms stand at attention, bringing my movements to a complete halt.

"Damn, Sam, I see you ain't playin' tonight, huh?" King said in a sexy, deep tone making sure his lips rubbed against my ear with every word. I smiled sexily because I was so happy it was him and not anybody else.

You know I had to play hard to get right. "Mr. James, what are you doing?" I asked as I pulled away slightly from his grip and turned around so we were looking in each other's eyes. He pulled me into him and placed his hands at the top of my ass, and I placed my arms around his neck. After a few minutes of us looking into each other's eyes, I broke eye contact and looked around to see who was watching us, because for some reason, I felt like someone was watching us, but nobody was paying us any attention. I tried to pull away and walk back over to the couches to get away from King, but he wasn't letting that shit happen. He pulled me back again, spinning me around so my back was to his chest, and wrapped his arms back around my waist locking me in place.

"Nah, you don't get to run this time, ma" he said into my ear, and immediately, I submitted. I relaxed my body into his and followed his lead. Once the song went off, we all headed back over to the VIP sitting area, and King pulled me down on his lap, locking me in place. For some reason, it made me feel uncomfortable, and my body stiffened. He looked at me and saw how uncomfortable I was, causing him to release the grip he had locking me in place. I slid my butt up on the thick arm of the couch and left my legs going across his legs.

We were all rocking to the music, and the vibe was nice as hell. Out of nowhere, King grabbed my chin and pulled my face over to him and kissing me directly on my lips. He pulled back, and when I looked into his low, lazy eyes, they were overrun with lust. I became so turned on that I grabbed the back of his head, pulling his lips back to mine, kissing him more aggressively than he kissed me. We kissed for what felt like five minutes before we came up for air. He whispered in my ear, "Damn, I want to fuck you. Right... Fucking... Now!" He kissed the side of my neck and then my ear.

From that point on, we were flirting heavy, but King decided to take the shit to the next level on my ass. He placed his lips on top of mine again, and out of instinct, I put my arms around his shoulders and deepened the kiss as he eased his thick hand up my dress at a snail's pace, teasing the hell out of me. I sucked his bottom lip in my mouth and sucked on it softly, then I bit down on it with my teeth. Not hard enough to draw blood but with enough pressure to get his attention. When he opened his eyes, I immediately sucked his tongue in my mouth, all while staring him down. Yeah, that's one of his weaknesses—his long ass tongue. Within seconds, his entire hand was up my dress. He parted my lower lips as much as he could and slid his thick middle finger inside of my wet hole. He didn't *move it initially but he just let them muthafuckas marinate in my pussy juices, and I was dying a slow death with every second that passed. I closed my eyes to brace myself for when he began moving his finger in and out of me. I got a little nervous and looked around and realized wasn't anybody paying us any attention.*

*"Ahhh!" I moaned out and leaned my head into the crook of his neck as King started to move his finger inside of me, in and out of me, at a slow and torturous pace.*

*He whispered in my ear, "Sam, open your eyes and look at me." But it took a minute for me to understand what he was saying because it was feeling so... damn... good. Suddenly, he stopped and slowly started to pull his finger out of me. I immediately opened my eyes and grabbed his hand, keeping it in place. "You know I don't like asking shit more than once," he said while circling my clit with his thumb.*

*I forgot he was into dominance and primal foreplay and sex, and it turned me on to the max. I knew the shit he did back in the day couldn't touch the shit he was doing now because back then, he was just coming into his own sexual identity.*

*He pushed his finger into me aggressively as hell while biting my fucking nipple through my dress. "Shit," I moaned out lowly I thought. Shit, at that point, I didn't even know or care who the fuck heard or saw something. My hips had a mind of their own because they started grinding into his finger. "Fuck, I'm about to cum. Fuck!" I began trying to kiss him, but he kept pulling his head back, licking my fucking lips. See, this nigga played too damn much. Shit, it was bad enough he had me in a fucking club getting finger banged, but he wanted to play games too. If looks could kill, he would have gone up in flames from how I grilled his ass. He removed his finger, tapped my leg so I would slide off his lap, and I did as he requested. He stood and walked into the bathroom in the VIP area. I sat there for a second, trying to figure out what just happened. Then it registered, and I began trying to talk myself out of getting up and going to get fucked in the bathroom of a club. Fuck it, I thought to myself.*

*I barely had pushed the bathroom door completely open before he pulled me in the bathroom by my arm and locked the door. He turned me to face the mirror, and we just intensely stared each other in the eyes for a few seconds.*

*King pulled my dress up, bent me over so I had a good arch, rubbed two fingers up and down my pussy a couple of times, and then he rammed his dick into me rough and hard. It was uncomfortable when he initially entered me because I hadn't had sex in a while, but thank God I was dripping wet from the foreplay on the couch. After a few strokes, it started to feel damn good. This nigga wasn't giving me back shots; they were spine shots. He was gonna have my ass poppin' wheelies in a wheelchair when he finished with my ass. I felt when he was finished, I would be paralyzed from the waist down.*

*King grabbed the back of my neck and pushed my face into the sink while making a growling sound right before he burst a big ass nut inside of me. Neither of us moved for about thirty seconds from trying to catch our breaths. After a minute or so, he pulled out of me slowly, and at that point, I was stuck and couldn't move. I heard him grab a paper towel, wipe himself, zip his pants, wash his hands, and head toward the door.*

*"I didn't get off! Where are you going!" I yelled mad as hell and almost in tears. He started laughing and walked back over to me, grabbed me around the front of my neck, and he stood me up so my back was to his chest, and we had a stare down in the mirror.*

*"I'm going back out to the party to enjoy myself. See I guess you forgot since it's been so long but I determine when that pussy releases and you don't get to release until I say you can... Don't worry. I'm going to take good care of her tonight," he said while tapping my pussy with his other hand a couple of times. I swear I never knew I would be into this kinky shit, but when he moved his hand, a mixture of his and my cum started running down my leg. "Yeah, I got that bitch purring, huh?" He laughed and released me and walked out the door leaving me there.*

We got a room at the Hilton downtown that night, and I had never been fucked in such an unorthodox manner in my life. He would be extremely rough, but at times. he was oh, so gentle. Up until that night. I had never squirted. but he had my shit squirting across the room multiple times. When we finally went to sleep the next morning, I fell asleep feeling safe in his arms and at peace for once in a very long time. When I woke up later that day, I could barely walk. but I wasn't even mad. I snuck in the bathroom and took a long and hot shower while King was still asleep.

While I was in the shower. I broke down crying because I knew when we walked out of that hotel room it would be the last time we could be together. Our beautiful night was over, and the worst part was we connected in a way that I felt only my husband should have had the capability of accessing. That scared me more than Brian ever finding out I cheated on him.

I was supposed to stay with Bennie and Moe for a week after the party, but I couldn't do it. I had to get away from Cleveland and King. I ain't gonna lie… Waking up in his arms was everything, and I knew if I spent any more time with him, I would want that to be my life, and at the time, it wasn't an option for either of us. Especially considering we were both married at the time. So after we left the hotel, and he dropped me off. I booked and caught me a flight back to Boston.

That was the first and only time I ever cheated on my husband. I thought by having the one-night stand with King, it would bring me some type of closure, but all it did was make me want to be with King even more. A couple of days after I returned to Boston, King called me numerous times, leaving message after message, but I never responded. After a couple of weeks of being home, I decided I wanted to be with King. I was happy as hell, but that shit was short lived because hours before I was going to call and tell him that, my doctor called me and told me I was pregnant.

As a parent, I felt I owed it to her to try and make our marriage work because I wanted her to be raised in a home with two parents that loved her unconditionally. I pushed the feelings I had for King to the back of my mind and threw myself into work and Brian until I had Kassidy, and my world was turned upside down. I cherished that one night I spent making love to King because the passion I experienced woke up parts of my body that I didn't even know existed.

# 8

# GETTING BACK TO BUSINESS

"King"

IT HAD BEEN a couple of weeks since I buried my one and only child. The pain I felt is something I couldn't even put into words. I can't begin to make you understand how bad that shit was hurting me. Only a person that's gone through it can truly understand the ache I felt in my heart all day, every day, and I felt like the man upstairs was punishing me for all the indiscretions I've committed over the years or something. *Who knows?* The only thing I really knew was, I wish I could take my son's place because no parent should have to bury their child.

The day Tammy told me she was pregnant with KJ was bittersweet. I wanted to be excited, but it was so much doubt surrounding the situation I couldn't be excited about the news. So I did what the average nigga did, I denied being the father.

It was no secret that Tammy got around, fucking different niggas to keep her pockets laced and bills paid. That was something she never denied when I asked her about it, but she said she was 100% sure KJ was my seed. I planned on having a DNA test done the day he was born, but after she pushed him out and the nurse put him in my arms, the paternity question went right out of the window. Our connection was instantaneous, so I canceled the test, signed the birth certificate, and became responsible for my little *prince*.

He brought so much joy and light to my world that was so cold and dark. KJ made me become a better man in a lot of ways, which in turn, made me an amazing dad. I wanted things for him I could never have when I was growing up, like two parents under one roof. That's why I married Tammy knowing I wasn't in love with her, but I felt I owed it to my son to at least to try my best to raise him in a two-parent household. I wanted to give him something I never had but always wanted growing up.

But the more time I spent away from Tammy, the more I realized how miserable I was when I was with her, and since KJ wasn't around anymore to be a buffer, I could see things for what they really were. I decided to have my lawyer draw up divorce papers and have her served by a carrier. I knew she had received them, but for some reason, she hadn't contacted me, which I thought was weird. I thought she would be banging down my door to get me to reconsider, but it was the total opposite.

I wanted to blame her so bad for my son's' death, but truth be told, if I blamed her, I would've had to blame myself too. I should have and could have taken him to the hospital when I realized her unfit ass had no plans on taking him. KDB business had me so damn busy, him being sick would slip my mind until I would go home at night and see him not feeling well. Knowing I could have possibly prevented him from dying was weighing heavy on my heart, and it was a mistake I wished I could go back in time and change. I couldn't, so it was a something I had to live with for the rest of my life.

I was so deep in grief I decided to take a couple of weeks off from business and grieve the loss of my son because mentally, I wasn't thinking clearly enough to handle any type of business. And in the drug game, not being focused on the task at hand could cause me to eat a bullet and not make it home at night. Envious niggas always trying to catch you slipping so they can take your place instead of putting in the work and building their own shit.

Since I had time off to just think things through, I started to question if the drug game where I wanted to be. My reason for doing it in the first place was so I could provide for my family, and since I don't have anyone to provide for, I didn't know if it made sense to continue on. The questioning was short lived when Preston Paris called me that morning while I was still wallowing around in my guilt and grief. He gave me a pep talk and made me see the bigger picture in the grand scheme of things, and I decided it was time for me to get back to business.

Preston Paris was like our boss in a way. He what I would call an OG and an Italian mob boss that's based here in Cleveland. His crew worked out of an area we called Little Italy, and Paris has his hand in everything illegal happening in Cleveland. We met some years ago after I helped his son get away from someone that was trying to kill him while we all were inside of Vision Blue, a lounge on Euclid Ave. I helped him flee the scene, and when we got about a mile away, I noticed he had been shot. I helped to get medical treatment, but he ended up dying a couple of days later from his injuries. His death caused Paris to do whatever he had to in order to find his son's killer, and Paris and I were both convinced it had to be an inside job.

Due to my background, he hired me to get him proof that it was an inside job, and once I did, he hired me to be one of his hittas. He gave me a twelve-person list to knock off, with specific instructions on how and when he wanted me to murder them because each person was someone from his organization who he suspected to be frauds. Paris needed their deaths to seem like someone on the outside of the organization killed them so he could keep his hands clean. I followed his instructions to the tee, and it took me exactly twelve months to kill everyone on the list.

During that year, Paris had me doing other things, and he took me under his wing showing me the ins and outs of all the business. I later found out the men I killed were ops that were helping the feds build a case against him, and the rest were just snakes trying to make power plays. Paris didn't know who could be trusted, so he also had me kill everyone on his son's team and started over with different people who he felt were trustworthy and would get the job done.

When I killed them, it opened up a position to become the main dealer here in Cleveland, and that's when Paris offered me the opportunity of a lifetime, making it almost impossible for me to say no.

Immediately after Paris offered me the position, I started the process of building my team, and Bennie was the first person I brought in. I knew if I was going to be out here in the streets, I needed someone beside me that I trusted wholeheartedly, knowing that they would give their life for mine. Once I broke my plan down to Bennie, he took what I had and made my original plan into some shit I could only come up with in my dreams. The second person I brought in was Keys because she was a muthafuckin' beast with coding and hacking any system, government included, without being noticed. I used her to help me find the evidence proving who was involved in killing Paris's son PJ, and like we originally thought, it was an inside job.

When Bennie joined forces with Keys, I knew we were going to make magic with those two geniuses together, and I knew anything was possible. They designed an amazing computer program that they combined with the transport system that we would use to transport our products to different locations. The system would run about 80% of our drug business, and it was something the drug game had never seen before.

It was crazy how when we broke down our plan to Paris, he was impressed, but he knew if we could make this work, we would change the drug game. He was also skeptical that we could pull it off, considering it had never been done before. Paris had been watching us closely since the first day we started selling work, giving us direction here and there and assisting with whatever we needed help with—like the district attorney, police commissioner, cops, detectives, and the mayor. He had so many people on his payroll, which meant we had the same people at our disposal, which we used to assist with building the corrupt foundation we needed so we could move how we needed to, to make the shit work.

During the first two years, things were a little difficult, and we were met with a little resistance, but that was because KDB was just being introduced to Cleveland's drug game. Paris watched us closely, making sure we didn't make any huge mistakes, but for the most part, he was happy with the progress we had made so far.

Out of the blue one day, when we were approaching year three, he approached Bennie, Damien, and myself about a proposition he wanted to offer us. He wanted us to be the plugs of the East Coast and eventually expand as needed, but we had to complete the revamping and initiation of the new transporting and distribution system we were completing. We estimated it would take us about a year and a half to two years tops to get things started and work out any kinks in the system. That was the main reason we were pushing so hard to get things done because we had a date set when we were supposed to start our transition into our new roles, plugging up Ohio, and all of the surrounding states.

When Paris called me earlier that day, I was at home wallowing away in my grief, and he wasn't having that shit. We addressed the problems I had been dealing with regarding the resistance Bennie was receiving, and he gave me a few suggestions on how he thought I should have handled things, but he let me know he trusted me to do what was best for the organization.

After the pep talk I had with Paris, it gave me the motivation to get up and get back to business, and that's exactly what I did. I knew we were short a man because Damien flew out to New York to secure a weapons deal he's been working on, so I decided to get dressed and head out to do a couple of pickups and just make sure shit running smoothly in a couple of spots we had been having a little trouble at.

I headed out and jumped in my car headed to one of our traps on houses on 129th and Arlington. I pulled up in an old-school, black, 1990 Chevy Impala with tinted windows, cut the car off, and instead of getting out right away, I turned my engine off and just watched the activity going on around the house. I hadn't shown my face in a couple weeks, so I just wanted to make sure everything was running properly. I looked around and saw niggas hanging out front like they at a kickback or some shit, and there were some young niggas I wasn't familiar with chillin' like they didn't have a care in the world. They were sitting on the porch with red Dixie cups in their hands, passing a couple of blunts around like they weren't at work, and it had to be our shit because I smelled it from three houses down. That shit was strong as fuck. As I exited my car, I grabbed my two 9mms from the hidden compartment up under the passenger seat, I checked the clips, and put one in the chamber of each before I exited my car. I walked up, and these young niggas started mugging me.

The youngest and dumbest muthafucka aggressively asked, "Is there a problem here, nigga?" I chuckled to myself because the little nigga had some heart. I wanted to take my belt off and whoop his little ass like Jody did the young nigga in *Baby Boy*, but I refrained from doing some retarded shit. To make matters worse, he had the nerve to say, "Bitch, I know you heard me. Do we have a muthafuckin' problem?" I assumed that was when everyone realized who I was because they started backing away from us with their arms in the air, indicating surrender. They already knew what it was, and they didn't want what was coming to their homeboy, because I was about to beat his ass and have fun doing it.

He started looking around with confusion plastered all over his face. I bellowed out a hearty laugh, and once I finished laughing, a cynical smile graced my face. I began pacing in front of him, and before I even realized what I was doing, I grabbed the nigga next to him by his neck, lifted his whole body in the air with his feet hanging about two inches above the ground, and then I dropped his ass to the ground. I kicked him in his side a few times, attempting to destroy his ribs, and I took my foot and stomped down on his chest like I was killing a roach. I grabbed the young nigga with so much mouth and commenced to whooping his ass. After a few minutes, I grabbed one of my guns from the back of my shorts and put my gun in his mouth, knocking one of his front teeth out.

"Now, bitch, what did *yooouuu* muthafuckin' say?" I asked, looking him dead in his eyes and pushing the gun a little deeper into his mouth.

I looked around for Chris, who was the lieutenant for this particular house, but I didn't see him. Main, who was Chris's right hand, ran outside and said, "King, I'm sorry! This my little cousin, Jason, and hell, we're both sorry for the disrespect my cousin showed you." I stared at him for a good twenty seconds because I was trying to decide what would be the best way to handle this situation. Main continued to beg for his people's life, but honestly, I didn't have any sympathy for his young ass. Main knew how I got down, and pulling a trigger didn't mean shit to me. I looked around, and everyone looked like they wanted to say something but were too scared to open their mouths. The neighbors started coming on their porches trying to see what was going on, so I decided it would be best for me to just put my gun up and let the little nigga breathe. I took the gun out his mouth and stuck my hand out to help him up. He took my hand and stumbled a little when he got to his feet, but before he was on his feet good, I rocked his ass, and he fell back to the ground.

"Don't you ever disrespect me again, because next time, no words will be spoken, just straight headshots. Do you fuckin' understand what I just said?" Jason nodded. I continued, "Know who the fuck you bossin' up to before you open your fuckin' mouth." I tried schooling the lil' dude because this is the first and last warning he would get from me.

"King, I'm sorry, man. This is my first time laying eyes on you, so I didn't know who you were. I would never disrespect you like that, my G."

"Y'all know this isn't how we run our shit, and we especially don't have muthafuckas outside hanging around like this the chill spot and shit. Clear this bitch the fuck out now! If you not on my payroll, get the fuck out of here, and don't come back unless you're making a purchase. I think some serious changes need to be made, because y'all niggas jeopardizing my establishment, which in turns jeopardizes my money!" I yelled. I needed to talk to Chris because he was fucking up... badly.

I headed straight for the room that we stored our work and money in. I punched the code into the keypad. It unlocked and popped open slightly. I walked into the green room and closed the door behind me, and it automatically locked back. Dolla Bill was putting money through the counter and rubber banding the stacks once they were counted.

"How the money looking, Dolla B?" I questioned, giving him dap, and then I grabbed a stack of money off the table that already had a rubber band around it. I shuffled my thumb through it taking a quick assessment of how much was in the bundle, and once I determined the amount, I laid the bundle back down.

"Man, can I speak freely without you getting upset and trying to whoop my ass like you just did Jason?" Dolla B asked, and we both burst out laughing. "But for real, King, the numbers aren't adding up and haven't been for the last couple of weeks. I had been following the chain of command by telling Chris, but every time I say something, he says he'll take care of everything. So that's just what I assumed he's been doing because nobody's approached me about it so far, so I thought that everything's copasetic. But I believe he's been taking money off the top, and either he's replacing it before Wayne picks up the money, or somehow, he's changing the numbers so y'all wouldn't find out. I have no clue how he could even change some shit though because Keys got shit on lock, but since money is my specialty, I feel like shit just not adding up.

"I just sent a text and call out to Damien and Bennie, but they haven't called back yet. I just don't want y'all to hold all of us responsible for some shit he's fucking up because we're doing our job. I know you've been dealing with a lot lately, but this shit crazy. That nigga barely shows up and works anymore. Main is the one that's been stepping up lately making sure things move properly. This shit right here can't fail, because this is how we all feed our fuckin' families, King, and I needs... my... money... man!" he said, sounding like Chris Tucker. If this was another time and place, I probably would have laughed, but I just couldn't.

"Well, Chris ass will be handled accordingly, and y'all know that's not how we run our shit, so he can't demote a second in command. His busta ass needs to quit cappin' because that's not how this shit works, and he knows this. This is one of the few houses left to be restructured and connected to the systems Hubb, so try to hang in there and take care of everything. The money you'll make in a week will seem like chump change, because you'll make that shit daily." I took a step closer to him, making sure he was looking in my eyes and giving me his full attention. "But this will be the first and last warning I ever give you pertaining to my money. If my money is fucked up in any way, it is your responsibility to inform one of us immediately. If you don't, I'm going to assume you have something to do with stealing my money. My nigga, you report to me!" I said to him loudly while poking him and then myself in my chest, further reiterating what I said. "It's a lot of shit I play about, but my money isn't one of them." I left him there to marinate on that little bit of information because I was the type of nigga to give a person only one warning, and then it's off with a niggas head.

I gave Main orders to shut the trap down and do an inventory count of the money and product that was stored there. Once they finished the count, they would transfer everything over to the Hubb when he goes for the emergency meeting we had just called.

It was crazy how I decided to take time off to get my mental right, and niggas start acting stupid. I felt it was time to show the non believers that shit wasn't sweet. I decided to head down to my condo so I could get myself mentally and physically prepared for the night's festivities because I already knew Bennie's crazy ass was about to be on some *good* bullshit.

# 9

# ONCE A CHEATER ALWAYS A CHEATER

"Damien"

KING, Bennie, and I decided in order for KDB to reach its full potential, we needed to change connects and start buying our weapons from the Russian cartel. The deal they brought to the table was way sweeter than what we had at the time, especially since Preston thought it was something he felt needed to be done. So when the Russians came to us almost a year ago and said they wanted us to take over the entire East Coast selling weapons, we jumped on it.

With the deal, we would get all our weapons cheaper due to the increasing amount of weapons we would need to cover the entire East. The quality of the weapons would be better, and the delivery method would change. Instead of our men driving to New York to pick up the weapons, the Russians would have them shipped to our harbor location here in Cleveland, and our men would pick them up from the harbor and drive the weapons to the Hubb. This change decreased the chance of any interference from the FBI or local police, and on top of everything, our profit would double from the increase in business.

That's why Romello and I were on our way to New York to meet with the Russians and finalize the deal. From what I could tell, we shouldn't have to be gone more than four or five days tops, but that was dependent upon how our new connect handled his business regarding new clients.

Main dropped Romello and I off at the airport two and a half hours before our flight was scheduled to take off for nothing. Our flight was delayed an extra hour, so we had a whole bunch of time to waste. When we finally boarded our plane, I needed a fat ass blunt bad and a drink bad as hell. As I got comfortable in my seat, I leaned back and closed my eyes waiting for the plane to pull off.

"Hello, sir. My name is Mya, and I'll be your stewardess up here in first class during your flight. Would you like for me to prepare you a refreshment or provide you with dinner or maybe a snack?" I heard our stewardess ask. I opened my eyes, and this fine, chocolate, thick ass goddess was standing next to me. I was so mesmerized by her appearance that I didn't answer her question right away because I was in a daze, staring at her until Mello elbowed me in my side, bringing me back to reality.

I cleared my throat, and then said, "Yeah. Let me get a Hennessy on the rocks please, Mya." I'm sorry, but a nigga a flirt and been one my whole life, and ain't shit going to change that. Miss Mya started blushing and shit, making me and Mello chuckle.

"Coming right up, sir," she responded. She made our drinks and handed them over. As she continued down the aisle, she made it her point to rub her thick ass thigh on my arm. She didn't know who she was fuckin' with because we both could join the mile-high club if that was what she wanted.

"Nigga, you don't think you're in enough fuckin' trouble? Flirting and shit. That's okay because Mill gonna cut your dick off, hand it to you, and then tell you to go fuck yourself with it," Mello said through laughter. I immediately grabbed for my dick out of instinct, but I had to admit he was right. "Have you told her about... you know?

"I'm still walking around alive, right? So hell no! I ain't said shit, but I don't want to talk about it right now," I said, aggravated as hell at myself because I put myself in the position I was in, and I had no way to fix this. I took a sip of my drink and savored the taste as it went down my throat because I was stressed the fuck out. It was like, in a way, I wanted to tell Camille myself about DJ and Chanel because the anxiety of waiting for the other shoe to drop had me feeling like I was getting a fuckin' stomach ulcer. But on the other hand, I knew telling Camille about my son meant the end of my marriage.

See, the shit was deeper than me just cheating on my wife. Chanel felt like she put in work just like Camille did to help me get to where I was. When I first started fuckin' with Chanel, I had also just started selling drugs, and I ain't gonna lie… I wasn't that good at it at first. My money would come up short, or I would have to use the money I made to take care of home.

So when I was short, Chanel would give me re-up money from time to time, and she also did other things to prove her loyalty to me. An example of that was when she set it up for me to buy a weapon from Wild Bill because I got robbed, and the niggas took my drugs, money, coat, and my Jordans off my feet, making me walk home in the fuckin' snow in socks. After that happened, I needed a gun to protect myself while I was on the block, and Chanel set that up for me.

The day I went to buy the gun from Bill, Chanel told me that he worked for her uncle, Julio. Chanel actually drove me to the spot I was supposed to meet Bill at, but before she got out the car, she told me to look out for her uncle because he would be in there, and he wanted to talk to me about a job. I was pumped as hell, but in the back of my mind, I was thinking the shit was suspect as hell. I walked into the building with my antennas up ready for whatever.

At an early age, I developed a love for weapons, especially guns and knives. That was something I got from my father because he was big into hunting, fishing, and things like that. He taught me everything I knew about guns.

When Bill showed me the guns he had available for me to buy, I looked all the guns over before I began handling the merchandise. Julio watched me break down the guns, load the guns, test the guns, question Bill about the guns, which he didn't have the answers to some of my questions, and Julio could tell I was very knowledgeable. Wild Bill and I were talking when Julio walked up, and he asked Bill to step out of the room for some reason.

Julio began talking to me, trying to feel me out. He asked me if I wanted to eat and if I was hungry enough to do what it takes to climb up in the game? I said, hell yeah! He told me how Bill was stealing from him, and if I wanted to take his place in the game, then I would have to kill Wild Bill.

I didn't say anything nor did I hesitate, but when Bill walked into the room, I picked up the gun that I had loaded and shot Bill between the eyes, and that was how I got into the weapons business. After I started selling weapons for Julio, word spread fast that Bill was out, and I was in. My name started ringing bells, and within a year, I had made a name for myself.

Maybe a year or so later, King approached me about a collab, and with me already pluggin' the city with weapons, King knew I could bring my weapons business to the table. So, he asked me to help him and Bennie get KDB started. I took him up on his offer, and we've been rocking ever since, and that's when my cheating went to a whole 'nother level.

Once I started bringing in that real money, became a co-founder of KDB, hoes started throwing pussy left and right. They would beg to suck the skin off my dick, and that was some shit I had never experienced before—bitches chasing after me. I was like a kid in a candy store, getting dome and fuckin' bitches left and right.

Camille always knew I was out here wildin', and she was cool with it as long as it didn't come to her and affect home. It seemed like bitches would be on a mission to bring it to her attention that I was out here cheating because hoes was petty and wanted what she had. They didn't know how to play their position. She would be pissed after finding out I cheated for a while and after a lot of begging and ass kissing, she would forgive me and let me come back home.

I remember at one time I had ten bad bitches on my roster that would be down to do anything I asked, but after a while, it was too much trouble, so I cut it down to two side bitches and random broads I would fuck with once and keep it movin'.

I ain't gonna lie... A couple of times I slipped up and got a few bitches pregnant, but I made sure them hoes got abortions because Camille was the only women who I wanted to carry my seed, and Chanel knew that. That was the reason she also knew I would have made her get an abortion if I found out she was pregnant with DJ. That was why she hid the pregnancy from me in the first place; I had already made her get two abortions in the past.

It's sad to say, but over the years Camille had whooped Chanel and other bitches' asses plenty of times. The last run in Camille had with Chanel was almost three years ago, and I can remember that shit like it was yesterday.

*Chanel pulled up on me at our trap on 129th and Arlington Avenue, which is the first trap we purchased and started running drugs out of. Before she got out the car, I knew she was going to be on that "leaving my wife" bullshit because she'd been saying it every day for about three weeks.*

*Chanel walked up to me, looking good, but I could see it in her eyes she was on some bullshit. "Hey, baby. Why you ain't been answering my calls?" Chanel asked. She kissed me on the lips and then smiled.*

*"I was working, and if I didn't answer your call, that meant I didn't have time to talk to your ass. Now can you get in your car and leave? I'll call you later when I'm not working." At that point, she was blowing up the spot all loud and ghetto as fuck. I grabbed her up and started walking her back to her car by force because she didn't want to leave for shit.*

*"Stop, Dame, you're hurting me! Let my fuckin' arm go, damn!" Chanel screamed. I was pissed the fuck off, and I didn't even respond, I just kept walking her over to the car because if I said anything, I would have had to yoke Chanel's stupid ass up.*

*We made it to her car, but before she could climb in, Camille pulled up and jumped out of her car. I knew my wife was going to be on some good bullshit because she had her hair in a ponytail, and she was wearing a jogging suit and tennis shoes. I knew she was about to get off in Chanel's ass.*

*Without saying a word, Camille grabbed Chanel's hair and pulled her away from me and the car like she was on a mission. That was when I real-*

ized what happened and why Chanel showed up here and how Mill knew where I was. Chanel was on some bullshit and somehow told Mill that we would be here together, hoping Camille would catch us doing something. See, this the little game Chanel loved to play, but I didn't understand why because she always ended getting her ass dragged by my wife in the end.

The look Mill gave me let me know if I intervened at all, it would start a war between the two of us, and that wasn't about to happen, so I let Camille get off in Chanel's ass a little.

"Yeah, bitch! I bet your ass won't slide in my DMs again, bitch, with your fake ass profile! Bitch, you ain't slick at all!" Camille yelled while stumping Chanel out. I had to stop it because Mill was killing her, and it looked like Chanel was inches away from taking a dirt nap when I was finally able to pull Mill away. Mill was like a raging bull trying to get away from me, and her strong ass was making it difficult for me to continue to hold her. If looks could kill, I swear I would be dead as fuck, that's how much anger and hurt was in my wife's eyes.

When I looked down at Chanel passed out on the ground, she wasn't moving, and hell, it looked like she was barely breathing. Her eyes were swollen partly shut, and her face was full of blood. I knew she needed to get to a hospital, and she needed to get there fast.

I was wrong as hell and should have been grabbed Camille off the girl, but I knew the more she took out on her, the less I would have to deal with at home later. I lifted Camille off the ground and put her over my shoulder and carried her over to her car. She had totally blown up our spot, so I knew I was going to have to shut shit down, and that meant we were going to be losing money for the day, which completely pissed me off.

When I got Camille in the car, I noticed one of our soldiers, Kurt, was putting Chanel into the passenger side of her car. I walked over to Chanel's car, and the sight before me made me gasp. "Damn, ma, she fucked you up," my silly ass said before Kurt and I burst out laughing. It was wrong to laugh, but she brought it all on herself. I stopped laughing and leaned into the car on the passenger side close to her ear and told her, "When you get to the hospital, tell them you didn't see who attacked you, and if decide to tell them my wife did this, I'm going to kill you, your mother, and your sister." Knowing her retarded ass, her pussy probably got wet from the words I spoke, but she knew

*I wasn't fucking around and to take my threat seriously because I didn't give a fuck. I would kill anybody—women, kids, and the elderly—about mine with no questions asked, especially when my wife's freedom was at stake.*

*Chanel started crying hard without responding, but I knew she understood what I had just said. I told Kurt to stay with her while she was at the hospital and to escort her home once she was discharged.*

*Before I could close Chanel's car door all the way, I heard a gun cock behind me. I put my hands up, showing a sign of surrender while looking up toward the house, and my niggas had their guns locked and loaded, and aimed at the person behind me. I already knew it was Camille because if it was anyone else they would have already bodied their asses.*

*I yelled, "Everybody, calm the fuck down and put y'all guns down!" I watched as everyone put the guns down with them resting at their side, and their index finger on the trigger ready to air that muthafucka out if necessary. Camille didn't budge.*

*Mill started screaming, "Why the fuck do you keep doing me like this, Dame! Cheating on me with these raggedy, tired ass bitches! I'm tired, and I'm done with your weak ass!" At the time, the only thing I was worried about was her shooting my ass. I trained Camille personally, so I knew she knew how to aim and shoot, and she was nice with a gun.*

*Suddenly, she started letting the fucking gun rip. I might be a savage ass nigga, but I was scared as fuck, real talk. Niggas were jumping for cover, and I couldn't do shit but stand there with my hands still in the surrender position, because if I moved, she was going to shoot my ass. She didn't stop pulling the trigger until the clip was fucking empty. As I was turning around, I saw she was replacing the empty clip and aiming the gun directly at me. My wife was official with a gun, and I knew the first clip was to scare me and Chanel, but the look in her eyes when she slid the second clip in really scared me. Her eyes were dark, and the tears had dried up. Her eyes showed anger and rage. Seconds later, I felt a burning sensation rip through my shoulder, not once, but twice. She didn't even wait for my body to hit the ground before she ran and jumped in her car and pulled off. Normally, when she was mad, she would throw her hands, but to actually shoot me is some whole other shit.*

*My shit was leaking bad as fuck, and I ended up passing out. When I came to, I was already at the hospital, and the doctors were treating my bullet* wounds. *The fucking cops were getting on my fucking nerves trying to get me to tell them who was the shooter. My thoughts just kept going back to my wife and how I was going to fuck her ass up once I was released from the hospital.*

*The entire ride to my house, King and Bennie were trying to keep me from going home, but they had me fucked all the way up in the worse way. I didn't give a fuck what we were going through; she shouldn't have upped that gun on me and pulled the trigger. I was her fucking husband and father to her fucking kids, and she could have killed me.*

*When I walked through the house, I yoked Camille's dumb ass up off the couch and began choking the shit out of her with my good hand. The grip I had on her neck was cutting off her oxygen supply, and she was about to pass out, but I didn't give two shits. The anger I was feeling wouldn't even allow me to say anything to her, so I spoke with my eyes.*

*A few tears rolled down both of our faces because I could have truly killed her at that moment. Eventually, King ran into the house and pulled me off her right before she passed out. Mill fell to the floor, gasping for air and grabbing at her neck.*

*I went to the bedroom and grabbed me some clothes and stayed at Bennie's for about two weeks. Honestly, I thought that was the end for the two of us. At the time, I thought it would've been best because there's nothing healthy about a husband and wife being seconds away from killing each other, but when my kids would come to visit, they questioned me about when I was coming back home, and that's when I knew I couldn't live without my family. I also took responsibility for the part I played in it, and that's what stopped me from fucking with Chanel for good, but you know the story didn't end there.*

*The day we both went to the hospital, Chanel ended up getting admitted for a few days. It was crazy because she was on my line days after getting out of the hospital to get some dick, but when I refused to come through and dick her down, things went left quickly. Since I had cut things off she wanted to hurt me by way of hurting Camille. She called the detectives and told them Camille is the one who attacked her, and she pressed charges, and she even told the twelve I threatened to kill her family. Camille was arrested and charged with assault with a deadly weapon, but we were able to get the charges dropped, but the damage had already been done.*

*Camille was angry with me for a long time and said she would never risk her freedom again because I couldn't keep my dick in my pants. She told me if I ever cheated on her again, she was going to file for divorce. That was one of the worse times we had as a married couple, and I promised myself and my wife I would never cheat again, and other than getting my dick and balls sucked from time to time, I was sticking to it. Until the devil came a knocking at my door fucking with me.*

About a year and a half ago, Chanel started calling and trying to get in contact with me, stating she needed to talk to me. Of course, initially, I was curving her for a little while, but then she sent a message that she wouldn't take no for an answer anymore because she had something important to discuss with me. I still didn't respond, so she kicked it up a notch and sent a picture of an approximately six-month-old baby boy in my DMs.

The wind was knocked out of me because he looked exactly like me when I was a baby. I mean, exactly like me. It was so bad he even had the same birthmark on his face like me, so in my mind, I didn't even need a DNA test to prove he was my son.

The night she told me about DJ, I was able to get away and sneak over to Chanel's to see him and talk to her about everything. I ended up staying over there late as fuck, getting to know DJ and developing a bond with the son I had always wanted. I fell asleep with him laying on my chest, and when I woke up and looked down at my son, it just felt right, but in the same breath, I knew him being here was going to end my marriage.

There was no way in hell Camille would accept an outside child, and what made things worse is my son's mother is Chanel. The person she hated the most in this world, and then my dumbass put the nail in the coffin for my marriage when I started fucking Chanel again. I know that was stupid, but being around her so much made a perfect storm for the shit to happen.

Somebody elbowing me in the side woke me up out of my sleep. "Aye, Damien, wake up. We just landed," Mello whispered. Once we retrieved our bags and made it to the rental car, I cut my phone on so I could send King and Bennie a text.

*Me: Landed! -D*

I sent Camille a message too.

*Me: I love you! -Hubbie*

I knew I wouldn't be able to talk to Camille until I got back to Cleveland, but I wanted her to know I loved her and let her know I was thinking about her, even though I was miles away. I cut my phone back off and got myself mentally ready to handle business so we could get our asses back home. I just hoped I had a home to go to when we finished in New York.

# SULKING IN HER SORROWS

"Sam"
*Twelve years ago*

ABOUT A WEEK AGO, *I was feeling nauseated all the time, sleeping every chance I could, and my stomach started to look like I had a beer gut because I was so bloated, and normally, my stomach was flat as a board. I snuck over to Moe's house and told her what was going on, and she suggested I take a pregnancy test because she thought I may have been pregnant, which was a possibility. King and I used condoms faithfully when we first started having sex, but as time passed, we became really careless, and I was getting scared I might have been pregnant.*

*I walked to Family Dollar and got a pregnancy test, and when I took it, the results came back positive quick as hell. What I didn't know at the time was a hating ass family friend saw me buying the test at Family Dollar. Time my cousin got home she call my mother and told her she saw me in the store purchasing a pregnancy test.*

*When I finally made it home that evening, my mother had a test waiting for me in the bathroom that she had gone out and purchased herself. I told her I didn't need to take the test because I already knew I was pregnant. She still made me take it, and of course, it came back positive, and my father walked in on us discussing the pregnancy test results, and that's how he found out I was pregnant.*

*He was so angry! He grabbed my mother by her hair and drug her out of the bathroom and into the hallway. He beat my mother for what seemed like hours, and when he got tired of hitting her, he took a break and then started in on me. He was slapping, punching, and kicking me in my stomach over and over again, and all I could think was,* he's going to kill me. *I knew what he was trying to do. He was trying to make me miscarry so he wouldn't have to pay for the abortion. I curled up in the fetal position to try and protect the baby the best I could until he tired his drunk ass out. Who the fuck does things like this to their flesh and blood? The fucking devil in human form, that's who.*

*The next morning, he had my mother call and she schedule me an appointment at Planned Parenthood, so I could get an abortion. I didn't know getting an abortion was a two-day process back then, and on day two is when I would get the abortion done.*

*A couple of days after I found out I was pregnant, I went for the first appointment. During that appointment, they confirmed the pregnancy, and I found out I was eight weeks pregnant. They performed an ultrasound, and when I heard the heartbeat, I almost died. To actually hear the heartbeat of the life inside of me broke my heart. At that point, I broke down and cried my eyes out. I wanted to scream from the hilltops that I wanted to keep my baby, but I knew my father would have murdered my ass that night. I knew I had no other option but to go through with the abortion and keep my mouth shut, but I didn't know how I was going to be able to deal with the fact I killed my baby when it was all over with.*

---

MY SECOND APPOINTMENT WAS FIVE DAYS AFTER MY FIRST APPOINTMENT, *and the entire ride to Planned Parenthood, I tried to get my father to change his mind, from the time we got to the car until he pulled in front of the building.*

*"Daddy, please don't make me do this! I want to keep my baby, and it's not fair you're making me kill it," I begged, but the request fell on deaf ears*

*because he wasn't hearing shit I was saying. Me and my father had been going back and forth about me aborting my baby since he found out I was pregnant the week before. Every time I said anything about it to him, I got my ass beat, but I had to try and save my babies life.*

*"Samantha, you must be crazy if you think I'm going to allow you to have a baby by that muthafucka. Hell! No! And don't make me repeat my mutha-fuckin' self. Do you understand me, Sam? You're running around here being a fuckin' hoe and shit, fucking anybody, showing your stupid ass a little fuckin' attention, but I blame myself. I gave you too much leeway, letting you go hang with that Moe girl. She's probably the one who's got you out here fucking." I was so scared at that point because the entire time he was talking we kept eye contact through the rearview mirror. It felt like I was looking into the eyes of the devil as I watched him scream at me, and I ain't gonna lie... I was scared as hell.*

*"After all this is done, I want you to cut ties with King and that fat ass girl, Moe, and if you ever tell anyone about what's about what's going on in my household, it'll be hell to pay for you. Do you understand me, Samantha?" I nodded my head up and down, letting him know I understood the threat he had just dished out. "If you disobey me, I will kill King and whomever else I need to, to make you understand I own you, Sammie, and King will never have you again." He made me so sick because now he began taunting me because Sammie was the pet name King gave me. "You're mine, now and forever. Now, little bitch, you can try and get out of having this abortion if you want to, but the blood of the people you love that's shed will be on your hands." He angrily scoffed while my mother sat in the front seat not saying a word. I just didn't understand how she allowed him to mistreat both of us like that.*

*I was so upset I hadn't even realized my father was pulling up in front of the Planned Parenthood building. As I looked around the parking lot, I could see protestors marching, holding signs with dead babies on it amongst other things, and I got terrified.*

*"Daddy, please don't make me do this," I begged once more.*

*"Get the fuck out, both of you! Renee, call me when y'all ready for me to pick y'all up. Sam, don't forget what I said will happen if don't go through*

with this." We got out the car and headed toward the entrance, and my feet felt like boulders were weighing them down.

I cried the entire procedure and the entire time I was in recovery. The nurse told my mother to keep a good eye on me just in case it becomes too much for me and I try to hurt myself.

As we walked out to my father's car, the sorrow I was previously feeling after the abortion was immediately replaced with hate and anger when I saw my father waiting for us inside his car. I hate this bitch, is all I was thinking with every step I made toward the car. Once I was inside the car, I leaned my head back on the headrest and began rubbing my stomach, thinking about the life I was just forced to kill. I felt so empty inside, and that made me so sad. I didn't want to give him the satisfaction of seeing me broken, but I couldn't hold it in anymore. I started crying uncontrollably. Normally "daddy dearest" would tell me to shut the fuck up, but he didn't say anything, surprising the hell out of me. Maybe he feels bad for making me get the abortion, I thought.

Once we made it home, I went straight to my room and laid down. I ended up dozing off from all the sedatives they gave me earlier at the clinic. My rest was short lived because my father shaking me woke me up. When I finally was able to open my eyes good, I noticed my father standing over me with our cordless phone in his hand.

"Get up! You need to call King and end the little relationship you have with him." He handed me the phone and leaned his body up against the wall and crossed his arms on his chest.

"Please don't make me do this. I'm sorry, and I won't have sex with him again, but I love him, and I need him in my life. Pleaseeee," I whined, but this bitch looked at me and laughed like I had just said a fuckin' joke.

"Make the fucking call. Now, Sam!" he yelled at me.

I picked the phone up and called King, and he picked up on the first ring, "Hello, beautiful. Why weren't you in school today? Baby, are you sick or something!" I got choked up from his concern of my well-being, but if he knew what I did earlier, he would hate my guts. King believed children were a gift from God, so to know I aborted his child would hurt him to the core, and that was something I refused to be responsible for. At that moment, I made the decision to take my secret about the abortion to the grave.

Softly through my tears, I said, "King, I think we need to break up. I need some—"

I couldn't even finish before his voice blared through the phone. "Sammie, why the fuck you playing with me right now? Did I do something to piss you off or something?" King questioned.

"No... I just need to focus on my studies. I can't do that while I'm tied down with a relationship. Please don't make this harder than it has to be," I begged while mugging my father's bitch ass.

"You got me so fucked up right now. What, I'm not supposed to try and fight for you or something? You're my fuckin' world, and I'm not letting you go... No, you can't break up with me!" he yelled. At that point I was crying so hard I couldn't even respond.

My father snatched the phone out of my hand and hung it up in King's face. "I don't want to see you around him or Moe. When you get out of school, come directly home, and if you do something other what I just said, they'll be hell to pay. Do you understand, Samantha?" he angrily asked.

"Yes," I whispered, and with that, he walked out of my room, leaving a sixteen-year-old girl to sulk in her sorrows.

# THE CALM BEFORE THE STORM

## "KING"

As I DROVE toward the Hubb, "Respect" by Jeezy blared through the speakers of my car as I got closer to my destination. I could feel the song in my soul because it described exactly how I was feeling. I treated everyone on our team like family, so for someone in our crew to feel comfortable enough to steal from me was rubbing me the wrong way.

"Ring, ring, ring," blared through my Bluetooth, interrupting my theme music for the night.

I answered the phone by pushing the button on my steering wheel and waited for Bennie to come on the

"Aye, King," Bennie responded. "How far out are you?"

"I just got off the freeway. I'll be there in about ten minutes. Why, what's up?" I questioned.

"Wayne had to run and handle something for me real quick before the meeting. I need you to do me a favor and go pick Sam up from Damien's real quick? I know you close, but I don't trust nobody else with my sister," Bennie explained. "I'll body one of these niggas over my sister."

"Yeah, I'll grab her," I answered.

Even though I was a few minutes away from the Hubb, I turned my car around, hopped on the freeway, and headed toward Dame's house to pick Sam up.

As I pulled into Damien and Moe's driveway, I parked my car in front of the garage and checked my surroundings making sure it was safe for Sam to come out. Everything seemed cool, so I pulled my phone out and sent Sam a text message, letting her know I was outside waiting for her.

**Me:** *Outside! -K*

**Sam:** *OMW out! -Sammie*

While I was waiting for her to come out, I logged into my Instagram account to see what was going on in the world of social media. A few broads I had fucked around with a couple of times in my DMs hollerin', but I wasn't on that shit because I had more pressing issues to deal with. I barely posted anything on social media. I would lurk around and like posts that I really thought was worthy of a "like". My head snapped up when I heard the front door close, and I watched Sam walk her sexy ass toward my car.

She climbed inside of my royal-blue Charger, buckled her seat belt, and leaned her head back into the headrest and closed her eyes. She didn't say a word to me, and for some reason, it rubbed me the wrong way. When you get into someone's fuckin' car, the polite thing to do would have been to say hello. I let it go and just backed out of the driveway, pulling off into traffic.

I decided to try and spark conversation to ease the silence tension, and hopefully, it would get her out of her head. "So Sam, how's life been treating you?" I questioned, looking back and forth between her and the road.

"It's been good. How about you?" she responded while still looking out of the passenger window.

"Life's been hard trying to adjust to a world that my son's not a part of anymore, but I'm finally starting to get things back on track... Aye, I want to thank you for everything you did for KJ when he was in the hospital and thanks for all the text messages and phone calls. I know I barely responded or answered, and I would like to apologize for that. I was just in a fucked-up mental space, and honestly, I couldn't deal with grieving and the feelings I still harbor for you at the same time."

If I was keeping it all the way one hundred with you, I stayed away because I felt like if I was alone with Sam, we would end up fucking. No ifs, ands, or buts about it because we had too much sexual chemistry between the two of us. Before we took it there again, I have some major shit I needed to get off my chest, and it was some questions I needed her to answer for me. The question at the top of the list is, why did she break things off like she did when we were in high school? That shit had been plaguing my mind since she did it, and I wasn't in the right headspace to have that type of conversation with her after burying my son.

She didn't respond immediately, but after I pushed her to go ahead and express herself freely, she chuckled, turned, and looked me in the eyes, and said, "It's funny how you can say you couldn't deal with your feelings for me because you were grieving, but you ain't too fucked up to fuck all these random, nasty ass bitches," and with that, she turned her head and started looking back out of the window.

Nah, what was straight bullshit is how instead of her saying you're welcome like a normal person would have said, she started going in on me for fucking "random bitches", and I got pissed the fuck off. I had been a ticking time bomb all day, and that was the catalyst that set me off. I knew I had to check her ass and get this shit out of the way.

"Wow! You don't give a fuck what comes out of them dick suckers, huh? First of all, Sam, you ain't my woman, so I shouldn't even respond to what you just said, but we can play your little game if that's what you want. Yeah, I fucked and will continue to fuck a bunch of random bitches, as much as I want to, and in a whole lot of positions. But the thing is… I can do that because I'm single, and the good thing about fucking a random bitch is there's no feelings involved, but with you, it's a lot of history and unresolved issues. So I fuck them bitches and send them on their way because they don't mean shit to me," I angrily spat. She didn't respond. She just leaned her head back on the headrest, crossed her arms on her chest, and closed her eyes.

The more I tried to calm myself down, the more I really analyzed the comment Sam threw out there. All I could get out of her little comment is that she was jealous because I was giving my good ass dick to someone other than her. Shit, I would be mad too because my shit was official and changed lives. I laughed on the inside before I began fucking with her to hopefully piss her ass off. "Jealousy doesn't look good on you, ma," I said in a sarcastic tone. She snapped her head around and gave me a death stare, so I continued on in a more aggressive tone, kicking it up a notch, knowing I was getting to her.

"Jealousy was laced all throughout your voice while you spurted that hot shit, but the facts still remain the same, you got a whole ass husband, and we're not together. And another thing, I would really appreciate it if you stop worrying about who box I'm knocking out," I said in an angry tone. The poor baby was mad, *mad*, pouting and shit! Her spoiled ass leaned her head back into the headrest and closed her eyes, trying to look like what I just said didn't affect her, but I knew better. Sam started squeezing those thick ass thighs together hard. With that I turned the radio on so I didn't have to sit in an awkward ass silence the rest of the way to our destination. Meek Mill's "Heaven or Hell" started blaring through the speakers. I turned the volume up just a little more and rocked his album the rest of the ride.

I pulled into my parking space at the Hubb and cut my car off. I looked over at Sam and realized she had fallen asleep. She must have been tired as fuck because the music was loud, and she still was able to fall asleep. I hated to wake her, but I had no choice. We had work to put in, so letting her sleep wasn't an option at that point. I shook Sam, and she awakened in a haste, looking around trying to figure out where she was, and once she gathered herself, we headed inside. I directed Sam up to my office, but as we passed a few crew members, one tried to hit on her. She ignored their advances and kept walking toward the stairs. See, this that disrespectful shit Bennie was talking about these niggas disrespectful as fuck, but that's OK because they were about to meet my crazy, and I bet people would be singing a different tune. I had been treating these niggas with kid gloves, and I think I did more harm than good by doing that.

Once we finally made it to my office, I keyed in my code, and the door popped open. Sam walked inside with me following behind her. I closed the door, and it automatically locked back. Sam walked around, checking out my office, which was a large size compared to some. What caught her attention was the artwork I had lining the walls. She noticed the artist's name on the plaque underneath it and ran her hand over it, realizing the name was of a guy we went to Glenville High School with. She didn't question it. She just moved on to the next piece. I had six different urban art pieces that lined the walls, and they were really nice to look at. My office was my oasis, and I designed it to be comfortable and homey because I spent so much time here.

I walked over to the front of my desk and leaned against it admiring the beauty in front of me. It was so much simplicity in her appearance, but it spoke volumes. She didn't have on any makeup, her hair was pulled back into a ponytail, she had on comfortable all-black attire—a plain cami or bodysuit and some yoga pants, Air Max, and a jean jacket. Even though it was a simple black outfit, Sam made that shit look so muthafuckin' sexy.

It looked like someone had sewn her into her clothes, and yes, the outfit was tight as hell. The bodysuit was little, and it looked like it belonged to her daughter how it was pushing her titties out the top, and then her nipples had the nerve to be hard as fuck. The tight yoga pants she had on with so much camel toe that I could tell she ain't have on no panties, and her pussy was hairless. *Fuck, outta here.* She knew what she was doing when she put that shit on, and I had to readjust myself discreetly when she turned around to plop down on the couch. Man, I could already tell… it was about to be a long ass night!

I needed a drink to calm myself down because my third leg had a mind of his own. I looked at Sam, and I could tell she needed one also by how nervous she was acting. I guess I wasn't the only one that needed something relax their nerves because she hadn't stop tapping her foot and playing with hair since she sat down on the couch.

Maybe she was still pissed because of what I said in the car, which she had the right to be because I was on one. What she said didn't warrant the response I gave her, and I can admit when I'm wrong. I wanted to apologize. I didn't want any added tension between us right now, considering what she was about to do. It was too much going on at the time for us to be at each other's throat, so I wanted to nip it in the bud before the meeting started.

I walked over to the bar and took a seat in one of the metal stools facing her. "Aye, Sam... I want to apologize for what I said in the car on the way here. I was wrong as hell and shouldn't have been taking my frustration with life out on you." She didn't respond or look my way, and she had this faraway look in her eyes like she was there with me physically but not mentally. I cleared my throat before I continued, "Would you like a drink to calm your nerves? I only have big boy drinks—some 1738, Patron, and Henny." I continued staring her down, awaiting her answer, but she took too long, so I just turned around and started preparing my drink.

I grabbed the bottle of 1738 and poured me a drink. When I looked back at Sam again, she still looked like she was not totally there, so I asked her, "What's up, you good, mama?"

It took her a second before she started talking, "Yeah. I just got a lot of shit on my mind. The last week, I've been trying to get myself mentally ready for this, so it's brought up a lot of bad memories I suppressed from my childhood. The shit my father made me do... was so fucked up. No father should ever do shit like that to their child."

She sat quietly for a moment, and then she said, "Yeah, I'll take some of whatever you're having. Hopefully, it'll calm my nerves down some, and I accept your apology, but you didn't have to apologize because I was wrong for even saying that shit. You're right. You not my man, but it's hard for me to think about you with another woman the way you've been with me."

I poured her a drink and walked over to the couch and handed it to her. She took the drink and gulped it down, wincing from the burn of the alcohol as it went down her throat, and then she stuck the glass out and asked for another one. I grabbed the bottle and refilled her glass, replaced the bottle on the bar, and took a seat next to her on the couch.

When I took the first sip, it burned so good going down, but this fool that was sitting next to me gulped her second drink down just as fast as she did the first one. I didn't know why she did that because 1738 is some grown-man shit, and she knew she was a lightweight. I knew in a few minutes, she was going to be drunk off her ass from those two drinks.

I turned on the couch so I was facing her, but she made it her point to look every way but in my direction. That wasn't gonna fly with me at all because above anything else, I felt Sam and I were friends before we became lovers. I grabbed her chin and turned her face so we were looking at each other in the eyes. The minute she blinked, the tears started rolling down her cheeks. I took my thumb and wiped the tears away, but it was useless because she started crying hard as hell, replacing those tears with more. I grabbed her glass and sat both our drinks on the table in front of us. I pulled her onto my lap, and she placed her head on my shoulder and wrapped her arms around my neck.

"First, let me clear the air by making something clear for you. I've never been with a female the way I've ever been with you because I've never cared about someone the way I care about you... but I'm getting a little worried, ma. How you acting, I feel like it's some other shit going on. Do you want to talk about it? You know I'm a good listener," I genuinely asked. I knew the shit with her father was really bothering her more than she was trying to portray because it would bother me if I was her. When we were a couple, she would never discuss the things her father did to her, so what I did know was from little things Bennie would let slip or what I assumed happened.

"Honestly, no, because some shit just hurts too bad, you know? One day, I want to open up and tell you everything because I feel you deserve that, but right now isn't the time to have that conversation, but thanks for offering to listen." She sniffled in my ear and pulled me closer into my body, and I did the same.

I rubbed my hand up and down her thick ass thighs, and I closed my eyes and relished in the feeling of having her soft body in my arms because it had been so long. I knew it wasn't the appropriate time to be thinking about sex, but damn it felt so fucking good. *It just feels right,* I thought to myself.

Sam moved her face, causing her lips to graze my ear, and when she did it again, I knew Sam was on some good bullshit at that point. She lifted her head, and we stared each other down like we were trying to see into each other's soul. I couldn't help myself. I leaned in and kissed her soft lips, which she reciprocated without hesitation.

Sam broke the kiss and positioned herself on my lap, straddling my body. As we kissed again, it deepened, awakening every nerve in my body. My hands had a mind of their own at that point as they started roaming her body starting at her tight ass. I gripped both her ass cheeks, pulling her closer into my body. My hands began moving up her back, and when I reached the small of her back, I came across a gun that was barely anchored down by her leggings. I immediately froze up and pulled my lips away from hers. She opened her eyes muggin' the hell out of me, searching for the reason I stopped the intimate moment. Sam hadn't even realized I had removed the gun from the small of her back.

"Why did you stop?" she asked curiously as she tried to peel away from me and stand, but I wasn't allowing that to happen. I pulled her back down and raised the gun up enough so she could see it, and a shocked expression grazed her face, but it immediately replaced with an expression I couldn't read.

I asked, "Do you even know how to shoot a gun?" She stared at the gun in my hand and then back at me and nodded her head. "Use your fucking words. You know I hate that shit."

"Yes, I know how to use a fucking gun." She jumped off my lap, grabbed the gun, chambered a round, and slammed it down on my desk. "What's the fucking problem, Kingston?" she asked while rolling her neck all ghetto and shit. It looked funny because that ratchet and ghetto shit wasn't even her.

I chuckled and said, "There's not a problem. I was just making sure you knew how to handle the gun you're carrying around. Nothing more or nothing less. Ain't no need to get all defensive and shit." I didn't want Sam to see how turned on I was by seeing her handle that gun with so much confidence and ease. My dick was getting harder with every second that passed. Her sexy ass had my mans rising to the occasion, and for some reason, I couldn't get my mind off of fuckin' the shit out of Sam.

I leaned my head back on the couch and closed my eyes, trying to think of anything that would calm the sexual beast fighting to get out. Sam walked back over to the couch and straddled my lap again. She slowly started trailing kisses from my ear to my lips, and we shared a kiss full passion and hunger. I broke the kiss and looked her in her eyes. I asked her, "Sammie, you sure you want to do this because I don't want you regretting this shit later?"

The seduction dancing in her big, beautiful, hazel eyes answered the question for me. *Damn, she's beautiful,* I thought to myself. She softly placed her lips on top of mine, and I deepened the kiss, adding some of my thick tongue. The kissing, rubbing, and grinding became almost animalistic how we were attacking each other.

I knew I had to have Sam, and I couldn't wait any longer. I ordered her, "Take your clothes off real quick because we don't have much time." I pulled my shirt over my head and threw it over the back of the coach.

Sam seductively began removing her clothes while I watched in a mesmerized daze. She slowly wiggled her yoga pants down her legs and then kicked them off once they were down to her ankles. She dropped the straps to the bodysuit one by one and slid it down her body and legs, removing it completely. She stood in front of me in her naked glory, looking like the beautiful, queen I had always known her to be and the sight that was in front of me had my dick hard and throbbing at this point, oozing pre-cum.

Sam pushed me down on the coach and straddled my lap again. I knew the lovey-dovey shit had to go out the window because I needed to be up in her gushy shit right then. My body and mind couldn't wait any longer, so I tilted my pelvis up a little so I could grab my wallet out of my pocket and get the condom I had stashed in there. Once I had the wallet in my hand, my concentration got sidetracked because

Sam pulled my dick out of my jogging pants, placed it at her pussy opening, and eased down on it slowly.

She released a loud, sexy ass breath once she made it halfway down. "Ahhh." My inpatient ass slid her completely down, and I held her there so I could get my mental right because I didn't bust within seconds. Sam's pussy was almost virgin tight, and I could tell either her husband's shit is little as fuck, or he hadn't long stroked her in a long time.

"*Damn,* ma, your shit tight as fuck. That nigga couldn't have been fuckin' your ass right at all." She didn't respond to my comment. She just started moving her hips in a circular motion, slowly and meticulously. I could tell her pussy was having trouble stretching to my size, and it was hurting her, but within a couple of seconds, I could tell she was able to adjust to my size. The moans she started to release let me know the pain had turned to pleasure.

I grabbed both of her breasts in my hands and squeezed them together bringing both of her nipples into my mouth at the same time. I sucked on her shit like a baby sucking on a pacifier. As I nibbled, pulled, and sucked, I could feel her pussy get wetter and wetter, making the feeling I was experiencing unexplainable.

"I haven't had sex in over a year if you must know," Sam moaned out. I was happy as fuck because that let me know she was probably completely done with her wack ass husband.

Sam pulled both of her legs up and placed her feet flat on the couch one by one. My toes began to curl once she started bouncing on my shit, and it allowed for my dick to slide in deeper into her tunnel. I bit my bottom lip to keep me from moaning out like a little bitch, but that shit wasn't working. "Fuckkkkkkk," I moaned out loud as hell. I leaned my head back on the couch and enjoyed her doing her thing for a few minutes before I stepped in because we had to speed things up.

I scooted my body down slightly on the couch while she was still ridin' me and told Sam, "Put your hands flat on my chest and raise up a little, ma." She did as she was told, and I slid my arms under her thighs and anchored her ass in my hands. I started slowly raising her up and down on my dick while fucking her from the bottom going deeper than before with every stroke, hitting the bottom of her box.

"Fuckkkkk, King!" she screamed, out loud might I add.

"Yeah, daddy deep in that shit ain't he?" I wasn't letting up at all, and when I sped up she collapsed on my chest, barely hanging on, so I repositioned my hands so I could continue.

Sam yelled out as the tip of my dick started poking at her G-spot, "Daddy I'm about to cum. I'm about to cum, daddy! Fuck!"

"Fuck... Me too. Let that shit go, ma. Let that shit go." Within seconds, her pussy started contracting around my dick sending me over too. "Gruhhhhh," I growled out. We both laid there breathing hard, eyes closed tight, trying to come down off our sex high.

Sam leaned her head back and kissed me softly on my lips and then went back to laying her head on my chest. After a couple of minutes, she eased off my lap, grabbed her clothes off the floor, and headed into the bathroom to clean up.

I stuffed my dick back into my pants and just sat there with my mind racing until she came out of the bathroom fully dressed. We didn't say anything to each other as I walked into the bathroom myself. After I cleaned up, I walked back into my office, and Sam was laying across the couch with her eyes closed. I asked, "Do you want to talk about what just happened?"

Without opening her eyes, she said, "Not right now. Just know I'm not regretting anything, and we'll discuss things later." With that, I walked over to her kissed her lips, and let her know somebody would be up to get her when we're ready for her. I walked out of my office to get the meeting started. I just hoped like hell I wouldn't regret sleeping with Sam after everything was said and done.

# SAVAGE ASS BEHAVIOR

## "BENNIE"

*January 15, 2016*

IT WAS *my second day back to work. I had been off for a month when my mother passed away. I struggled a lot when she died for some odd reason, but I was finally in a good place mentally. I had been at work in the emergency room department, working for a couple of hours, and I grabbed a chart and walked into the room of the next patient I was treating. As I started my physical exam, someone knocked on the door, immediately stopping the exam.*

*"Dr. Howard, can you step out into the hallway, please? It's very important," Diane asked calmly.*

*"Sure. Sir, can you excuse me for a minute? I'll be right back," I explained to the patient before walking out to see what she wanted.*

*Once I made it into the hallway, Diane was nowhere to be found, so I walked toward the nurse's station. When my presence was made apparent to everyone, they looked at me with saddened eyes. Diane motioned for me to follow her into one of the consultation rooms because two cops were there to talk to me. The entire time I walked over to the room, I was thinking they wanted to talk to me about one of the GSW patients I had earlier, or something like that, but when I opened the door, I saw two uniformed officers, King, Damien, and Wayne. They were standing there trying their best not to* make eye contact with me, and that's when I started getting concerned. It could have been about a KDB member, but if it was, none of them would have shown their face here, so that wasn't it. I knew it had to have something to do with someone in my immediate family, but which one?

I asked, "What's going on?"

Everyone looked at each other before the cop started speaking. "Hello, Mr. Howard. I'm Detective Edwards," he said as he held his hand out for me to shake, which I ignored, and eventually, he dropped his hand. Normally, I was not like that, but this cop was rubbing me the wrong way. Plus, I knew he's about to tell me some bullshit I didn't want to hear. "Well, um, sir, I'm here to inform you that your wife, Monique Howard, was involved in a car accident, totaling her car. She either lost control or passed out behind the wheel and hit a telephone pole. She was unconscious when she was brought here for treatment, and the surgeons just rushed her to the operating room because she has some internal bleeding."

As I stood there staring at him, it finally registered what he had just said. I turned and grabbed the knob to rush out the room because I needed to go upstairs to the surgery and see what the fuck was going on, but King screaming stopped me from turning the knob and opening the door.

"B, it's more! Everybody except Damien please leave so we can talk to our brother and tell him the rest privately," It seemed like everyone was happy as hell they had an excuse to leave and not have to deal with the fallout from what I was about to be told.

"What the fuck is going on, King?" I asked aggressively, getting upset.

"Well, I'm just going to say it... Fuck... the kids were in the car with Moe, and man—"

I cut King off and yelled, "What!" When I looked in King's eyes, I knew the look he had all too well because I've worn it plenty of times when I had to tell people their family member died.

"Ben, it's not good, bro. They brought Jessica in with Moe, and she was rushed to the operating room too, right behind Moe." King stopped talking and started looking at the floor and then over at Damien. When he looked back up and gave me eye contact tears were threatening to fall from his eyes. At that point, I knew BJ didn't make it.

All I could whisper out is, "Please don't tell me BJ didn't make it. King...

*King... Please don't tell me my son is dead." I looked over at Damien to see if I could see a hint of this being bullshit, but he wouldn't even look at me. "Dame, please tell me this nigga lying. Please tell me he's lying." Damien and King both shook their heads side to side, letting me know it wasn't a lie.*

*"I'm sorry, B," King kept repeating over and over again, and that's when I completely lost my shit. I started throwing chairs around the room, flipped the table, and punched two holes in the walls before King was able to grab me in a bear hug from the back and subdue me. Once I calmed down, I finally walked out of the room, and I ran right into security, but they could tell I was in that "wish a nigga would" mode. How I felt, I might have aired the mutha-fuckin' emergency room out. I had to check and see how Jessica and Moe were before I lost my damn mind because they were all I had left.*

*Jessica ended up dying on the operating room table, and Moe survived, but she ended up miscarrying a baby we didn't even know she was pregnant with. We were trying to get her pregnant and would have loved that child just like we loved our other two, but all our children were tragically taken away from us.*

---

FOR DAYS, I HAD BEEN STRUGGLING WITH THE FACT THAT MY FATHER raped my fuckin' wife and how she ended up wrapping her car around a pole trying to get away from him, which caused the death of our children.

It finally made me understand why she was acting the way she did after the dust had settled following the accident. In a crazy way, I thought the revelation would bring us closer together because we both went through traumatic experiences by the hand of my sperm donor, but instead of making things better, it made things worse for me. No matter what I did, I couldn't get the image of my father raping her out of my head, and I couldn't bring myself to tell my wife that was the real reason I couldn't have sex with her because I know it would hurt her to the core. So I had been avoiding her ass like the plague.

I think she started to sense something was wrong because of how I was acting. I made sure I didn't go home until I knew she was asleep or not home. Whenever I would get home, I would sit in one of the chairs in our bedroom and watch her sleep. I know that sounded a little stalkerish, but that was not the case.

One night when I came into the bedroom, and she was asleep, she started having a nightmare, so every night since then, I would watch her sleep, and whenever she had a nightmare, I would get in bed and hold her until she calmed down and got back into a deep sleep. After I knew she was good, I would go to the guest room and go to sleep.

I just couldn't wrap my mind around my wife telling me my fucking father raped her, and he was the reason she had the accident that killed all my seeds. I had always had a hunch that it was more to the story because shit just wasn't adding up, but I couldn't understand why. I let it go because she struggled so bad afterward, and I didn't want to make things worse for her, but to know that nigga violated her in that way was killing me. But one thing was for sure, he would never hurt my wife or my sister again, and I couldn't wait to handle his bitch ass, but patience was a virtue with this situation. I had to handle his death in a particular way so I could maximize on his death in more ways than one.

Dealing with Moe's confession about the rape, the shit my father did, my job duties as assistant director at the hospital, and KDB business had me stressed the fuck out and tired as hell. It seemed like the days started running into each other, and I didn't know if I was coming or going, especially considering I was only getting maybe three to four hours of sleep at night. Then to make matters worse, the shit that went down on 129th earlier that day caused King to shut down that trap, costing us all money.

That's the reason we decided to call an emergency meeting and iron out the wrinkles with the crew. We didn't want to do it while Dame was out of town, but shit was getting out of hand. The problem was niggas just kept doing dumb shit because King hadn't been showing his face lately, and then I stepped in, taking over his duties without being formally introduced beforehand to everyone, making them look at me sideways. The crew knew of me, but most hadn't met me. In the past, I had only dealt with our lieutenants and Wayne, Dame, and King dealt with everyone else. We were going to wait to introduce me to the team, but the things that had transpired over the last couple of days got me side-eyeing every fucking body and trusting only a few. So we had to do the introduction sooner than we wanted, but it was necessary.

When Wayne picked me up for the meeting, so many things were running through my head, but mentally, I was exhausted and just wanted to get the meeting over with so I could I go home and get some fuckin' sleep. The meeting was being held at our organization's central location, the Hubb.

The Hubb was an old, abandoned factory we transformed into the core of our underground transportation system. The location was where we stored our weight, guns, and whatever other products we used. We held all our meetings there and whatever other things that needed to be handled regarding KDB business, and the front of the building is where we ran our legal businesses out of, but that was more of King's lead than mine.

When I initially went to Keys about the ideas I had for the transporting and drug dispensing system, we both didn't think we could find a way to make my vision a reality. It was crazy how I even came up with the idea to use the tunnels in the first place. One day, I was down at the mayor's office for a meeting and noticed a diagram showing the development of Cleveland. The diagram had pictures of the underground tunnels and how they used it to transport their equipment from location to location. I asked a few questions and did some research and realized how we could use the tunnels to transport our product and weight undetected.

See, the original reason the tunnels were developed back in the early 1900s was so they could use the tunnels to help assist city workers with transporting materials they were using for the production of the sewer and water system throughout the city. The system was used for approximately fifty years, and in the 1970s the city decided to close the system due to the upkeep being too expensive. Plus, cheaper solutions were developed by this time to assist with maintaining the sewer system. The tunnel system had been abandoned and forgotten about up until we decided it would be an asset to our team.

Once the mayor signed off on us using the tunnels, and we took possession, Keys and I went into go mode and developed a program and computer system that allowed Keys to run everything from the Hubb with only needing a few workers at the houses to assist with the dispensing system. It took us months to develop a blueprint for the system and then another couple of months to figure out how to make it happen and find a construction crew who could pull it off. Even though things weren't going exactly as planned, progress was still being made, and since the project was so complex, I wasn't upset.

After walking into the Hubb and getting an update on the transporting project, I headed straight to my office to prepare myself for the meeting that was about to start shortly. I wasn't in my office fifteen minutes before King notified me they were ready to start the meeting.

"B, we're ready to start the meeting," I heard King say through my walkie-talkie.

"I'm on my way down," I replied while locking my personal belongings up in my safe, and I headed downstairs to get the meeting started.

Immediately, when I walked into the conference room, I scanned the room, sizing up the men, trying to get a read from everyone. I had only dealt with the lieutenants, so most of the men looking back at me didn't have a clue who I was, but best believe I knew who they all were. I walked across the room to take a seat next to King.

As I was sitting down, I heard someone mumble under their breath, "Who the fuck is this nigga?"

Before I could even say anything, King leapt out his seat and snatched the kid up out of his chair, throwing him to the ground. King started repeatedly punching the dude in the face, over and over again. Each punch had so much power behind it that you could hear cracking noises from bones breaking. After a couple of more blows, King dropped dude's body to the ground and walked away from him.

King started shaking his right hand, the hand he was punching him with. I couldn't do shit but hope he didn't break it because from where I was standing, I could tell his knuckles were swollen and red. He looked up, giving everyone direct eye contact, intimidating the hell out of the room. I couldn't do shit but chuckle because I thought I was going to be the one out of control and on some good bullshit, but I guess they get two for the price of one.

King grabbed his gun from his waist and then commenced to beating the breaks off the nigga who ass he had just beat with his fist, but at that point, he was beating his ass with the butt of the gun. King finally stopped and looked at his hands, and they were a bloody mess. He laid the gun on the table, took his shirt off, and cleaned the blood off his hands with it and returned his gun to his waist.

I looked down at dude, and you couldn't tell if issa man or issa woman because he was so fucked up, but that ass whooping was well deserved. I began observing the men's facial expression and body language. Rage started taking over because a few men in the room looked scared shitless, and fear was oozing from their pores. That gave me the confirmation I needed that something had to change. A few niggas in there would no longer be representing KDB at the end of that meeting. Shouldn't no man on our team ever show fear of another man, and for some reason, seeing the fear in a few of their eyes was really rubbing me the wrong way.

King yelled out, "Let me say this first, nobody was supposed to be fucking talking because the meeting had started! I can't stand a disrespectful muthafucka. Now, it has been brought to my attention that you niggas been truly wildin' since I had been off, grieving the loss of my *seed*." King kicked the dude—who's ass he had just beat—in the face, rendering him unconscious, but at the time, I thought he might have been dead.

"Y'all niggas need to get it through y'all thick ass skulls we see everything muthafuckin' thing, so all those muthafuckas will be handled accordingly! Also, a few of y'all niggas ain't built for this shit, so we'll be revoking your membership at the end of this meeting!" Wayne yelled angrily, looking like a pit bull ready to attack his prey.

I stood and began addressing the room. "Well, everyone, we felt it was time I introduce myself to the team. I'm one of your leaders, and y'all address me as B, or Beast. I want to share a motto I live by, and I really want you to think about the words: Any man can be given the title of king, but a *real* king earns his title, and that's exactly what we did. We earned our titles as Kings and leaders of KDB, and y'all have to earn your titles as members. We put in the work to get us where we are now, and we expect y'all do whatever needed to take this organization to the next level.

"My primary focus from here on out will primarily be on the drug distribution side of things, and I'll still be working with Wayne as my right hand. You all know we have a chain of command, so if any of you lieutenants have a problem, address it with Wayne, and if it's worth me addressing, I will. All lieutenants, please report here tomorrow at noon. We're going to change a few things from here on out.

"That's all I really have to say, for now. This was just an introduction and also a warning to let y'all know we see all things, so move accordingly. If you feel like this ain't for you, bow out gracefully. After tonight, the only way out is a bullet between the eyes. King has been too nice to you muthafuckas, real talk. Just know I'm not King, and you are responsible for your actions. This is my one and only warning that I'll give you. I have no tolerance for bullshit, and I have zero fucks to give," I warned our team.

I looked around just to make sure I still had everyone's full attention. "When you arrived, I instructed the lieutenants to give y'all a tour because for most of you, this is your first time here, and I would like for everyone to follow me because we saved the best room for last." I stood, and everyone followed King and myself into the workroom.

Once everyone piled in and started looking around, I looked in the camera and gave Keys the signal to lower the chain from the ceiling. When the ceiling doors started to open, everyone looked up, confused at first, but when they saw the naked body being lowered, they figured out real quick what was about to happen. I truly hated going to the place I was about to go mentally because afterward, it was hard for me to readjust back to myself, but some things can't be helped.

It was crazy how my whole demeanor changed. My heart rate increased, my thinking and analyzing was different, and I felt like I had no physical restrictions. My therapist, Kelly Winters, said she felt I made up the Beast personality as a defense mechanism when I was being abused by my father. She said that was how I was able to make it out of that house halfway sane because the Beast personality took the abuse, not me.

As we all watched the man be lowered down and his feet stop about two inches from the ground, he kept jerking around, trying to release his hands from the chains and scream through the tape. A cynical laugh escaped my lips, and then it deepened, coming from my gut. My dick got hard thinking about all the pain I was about to inflict on his ass, and I barely was able to contain myself.

"So I know you're wondering who's the mystery man hanging from the ceiling and what the fuck did he do? Right? Well, this man violated and took something that didn't belong to him. I'm going to make sure he pays for all his fucked-up discretions he's committed over his lifetime. Shit, I'm the judge and the jury right now, and he's been sentenced to death." I looked up to make sure I had everyone's attention still, which I did, so I turned and looked into the camera and sent a signal to Keys to open the hidden sliding door on the wall that revealed all the toys I placed in there. It was hard for me to decide which weapon I wanted to start with, so I studied the tools for a few seconds, feeling like a kid in a candy store.

I put on a pair of leather gloves and grabbed two steel bats from the wall, whirling them in a circular motion, causing everyone to take a few steps back. I commenced to beating this nigga's ass until my biceps hurt from me bringing the bat up so high and bringing it down on the nigga's body so hard. All while I was beating him, I could hear his bones breaking just like I wanted them to, which caused me to smile on the inside.

The more adrenaline that pumped through my veins, the angrier I got, causing me to have flashbacks and see images of all the things this man had done to me, my sister, my kids, and my wife. I threw the bats on the ground, punching him with powerful blows all over his body. With every hit, his body would fly away from me then it would fly back like a punching bag, and that was how I treated it.

I could feel someone wrap their arms around my upper body, which prevented me from swinging anymore. I heard King speaking, which pulled out of the dark mental space I had gone to. "Ben, calm down, bro. Calm down, bro!" I snatched myself out of King's grasp and took a few steps backward and started pacing, trying to calm myself down some.

I stopped pacing because I calmed down enough to address the team. "Oh, yeah, I think I forgot to tell y'all this is my dear old father… Bitch, wake the fuck up and tell King what the fuck you did, and don't leave shit out! Tell him everything you told me earlier because this shit affects him just as much as it affects Sam and me."

"B, what the fuck are you talking about?" King questioned with a confused look on his face.

Before I could respond, someone to the right of me whispered, "These niggas crazy as fuck!" I looked over at him, and King sent a hollow point straight between his eyes, and his body dropped to the ground with a loud thud.

"Damn! Would anybody else like to say anything!" King yelled while waving his gun around, and nobody said one word. "You know what? Everybody get the fuck out of here!. Now!" King yelled, and them niggas started running out of the workroom like this bitch was on fire.

"Well, um… when Sam was about ten, I started noticing she was at the beginning stages of becoming a woman. Initially, it started out with me watching her walk around in her pajamas, and then she started her period, becoming more feminine, and she became more attractive to me. Then she would walk around in little ass shorts and tight shirts without a bra on, teasing me, so that was how I knew she felt the same way about me as I felt about her.

"When she turned fourteen, I couldn't take it anymore, and I had to touch her. She was scared initially, but I told her it was how daddies showed their daughters love. A couple of times, I had to threaten Bennie and their mother's lives if she ever told anyone to keep her quiet. She would kiss me and tell me how much she loved me, and she wanted me just as much as I wanted her. King, after y'all start dating she had less and less time to spend with me, which pissed me off.

"Eventually, one day, she told me she loved you, and she wanted me to stop touching her because she thought it was wrong. I told her I would stop if she allowed me to spend one day with her, and I could do whatever I wanted. She agreed to it, but when I inserted my finger into her, something was different, and I could tell she wasn't a virgin anymore. She told me y'all had sex and that she was in love with you. I was infuriated so I told her if she wanted to be a hoe so bad, I would make her a hoe." Steam started coming out of King's ears and tears started rolling down his face, which caught me by surprise. I had only seen King shed a tear maybe once or twice. Once when KJ died and at his funeral. That's it, so to see him to drop tears for my sister let me know how much he really loved her.

My father was a sick son of a bitch! It was blowing me is how my father explained what he did to his daughter like she was just another bitch he fucked with. He didn't even go in detail like this earlier when we transported his pedophile ass here. If I knew he was going to say all of that, I would have never asked him to tell King shit. *Fuck!*

He explained what happened like his sick ass was reading a story out loud from a book. He got all dreamy eyed and shit whenever he would say Sam's name. This sick shit had my stomach turning, and I felt like I was about to throw up. I was a ruthless ass nigga, but this my sister, my fucking baby sister at that. The shit he said started to mess with me mentally, and I wished I could have unheard everything he had just said.

"She told me she was pregnant by you, King. Shortly after that she said she wanted to have an abortion and asked would I pay for it. Her mother took her to have the abortion, and I paid for it, but she was different after that. She hated my guts and wouldn't say more than two words to me at a time. I used to get so mad, and I hated that I would take my frustrations out on her.

"Sammie was supposed to love me, not you, King. You didn't give a fuck about her... I had asked God to forgive me for my sins, and I hope one day Sam can too. I'm a sick, old man, and I don't have much time left, but I'm sorry for what I had done. King, I'm sorry I made he—"

Before he could finish his apologies, King two pieced his ass and then threw a mean uppercut Max's way. His lying ass ain't sorry. He was trying to confess his sins, hoping he would get forgiveness from the good Lord and be allowed safe passage into heaven when he crossed over. I just prayed God wouldn't allow his fake ass into His holy gates because he wasn't remorseful for all the bad things he did to others with his pedophile ass. I wasn't worried because I was confident it was a warm, cushy spot in hell waiting just for his ass.

"This nigga ain't sorry because if he was, he wouldn't have raped Moe when my mother died. Bitch ass nigga!" I yelled, fuming. I started pacing in an attempt to calm myself down a little before I became completely unhinged, and that wouldn't be good for anybody.

You could feel the rage and anger in the room consuming King and myself. Within a blink of an eye, we both started throwing haymakers at his ass. Punch after punch, face and body shots, which caused blood to squirt everywhere from his face. We knocked him clean the fuck out again. I motioned for King to stop hitting him for a second so I could grab another ammonia inhalant packet. I snapped it in half and placed it under his nose. Max woke up immediately with his eyes wide as hell, looking around to see what was going on.

I yelled, "Nah, bitch, you ain't crossed over yet! Wake that ass up!"

I grabbed my Elk Ridge knife in one hand and a special blue box off the table housing the tools I pulled earlier and started walking back over to my dear old pops. Before I could do anything else, I turned to King and asked him, "King, I'm about to turn this shit up a notch. Are you staying or going, 'cause this shit I'm about to do may turn your stomach with your soft, pussy ass?" I chuckled briefly in a cynical manner, enjoying the fact that it was time to wake dear ole daddy back up.

I placed the special box on the floor, grabbed another ammonia inhalant, popped it, put it under his nose, and again, he woke up screaming with wide eyes. Once my father was back with the living, I took the knife and sliced the tip of his dick off, and then I skinned the rest of his dick like it was a fish, which caused Max to wake up out of his sleep screaming.

It was funny because he went from snoring to screaming, crying, sweating, and then passed out again. He had me fucked up though because he was going to be up for all of this torture, and he better enjoy it. Again, I grabbed an ammonia inhalant, popped it, put it under his nose, and again, he woke up screaming. Once he was back, I grabbed the blue box and poured a handful of salt in my hand. It wasn't simple table salt, but I was using coarse salt that has a higher salt content. I grabbed his dick in that same hand and squeezed it so the salt can settle on it. He let out blood-curdling screams, and I swear his screams had to go up an octave.

"Bitch, shut the fuck up!" I yelled.

He started begging for me to stop in between his screams, and that shit fell on deaf ears. "Did Moe beg you to stop when you raped her? See, you fucked up when you touched something that belonged to me. Yeah, you really fucked up!" I taunted him with spittle coming out my mouth, landing on his face. I reached down in my soul and pulled up the thickest and largest amount of phlegm I could muster up and spit it right in his face. All I could think about was how much I hated his bitch ass!

"Bitch, you don't get to sleep during this!" I screamed with anger raging through my body. I noticed he had blood leaking down his leg onto the floor at a fast rate. I grabbed the small torch and cauterized what was left of his dick so he wouldn't bleed out. Nope. He wasn't going to bleed out nor would I allow him to die before I was done. If I had to start an IV on him and give him blood, medication, or whatever else I needed to do to keep him alive.

He started screaming and pleading and begging for me to stop, but that wasn't going to happen because the fun was just getting started.

"Ben, I'm so sorry for what I did to Moe. I swear I didn't know my grandkids were in the car." Those words stopped me in my tracks and the memories of my kids hit me like a ton of bricks, and I was stuck, causing me to drop the knife. For this bastard to even let that shit come out of his mouth took my anger to a whole new level. I walked over to him and punched him over and over again in his face, knocking a few teeth out of his mouth. I walked back over to the table where the knife was laying and picked it up twirling it in between my fingers.

I stopped twirling the knife after a couple of seconds and threw the knife in the air and caught it between the palms of my hands. I did it again and watched as it came down, and when it was close enough for me to catch, I caught the knife and threw it at my father. It landed exactly where I wanted it to—in the dead space where his heart should have been located, with his heartless ass.

I knew long as the knife stayed in place he wouldn't bleed out. I looked behind me for Wayne so he could go grab Sam out of King's office because I was ready for the shit to be over with. "Aye, Wayne, can you go—"

I couldn't even finish my request because Sam walked into the room and straight up to our dear old pops, raised a nice ass 9mm, and emptied the clip in his chest, stomach, and a one-hitta shot to the head right between his eyes just like I taught her. I swear I felt like a proud parent right then. She came in, fucked some shit up, and then dropped the muthafuckin' mic.

Sam stood in the same place for about five minutes before she walked over to King and attempted to wrap her arms around his waist so he could console her, but King curved her and continued pacing the floor. She looked over at me with tears running down her face, silently asking what's going on. I just shook my head from side to side, letting her know to let the shit go for now, but she wouldn't be Sam if she would've done that. I knew then shit was about to go left, and I prayed I didn't have to fucking shoot King for putting his hands on my sister.

"King, can you explain to me how not even an hour ago we were fucking in your office, and now you don't want me to touch you?" she angrily asked. King stopped pacing, turned, and looked at her with so much disgust and anger in his eyes and face.

"Sam, I suggest you leave and let me calm the... fuck... down!" King screamed in her face with spittle landing on her face while pointing at the door.

I walked over to them and stood in between the two, so my back was to King, and my chest was to Sam, blocking King from being able to touch her. I grabbed Sam by the arm and tried to gently guide her out of the room, but she snatched away and ran back over to where King was still pacing.

"King, what the fuck did I do, huh? What did I do?" Sam hysterically cried out.

King stopped pacing and rushed over to Sam and grabbed her by the throat, squeezing hard as fuck and yelled, "You killed my mutha-fuckin' seed, bitch! That's the fuckin' problem!"

**\*\*\*\*\*TO BE CONTINUED\*\*\*\*\***

**Have You Grabbed This Yet?**

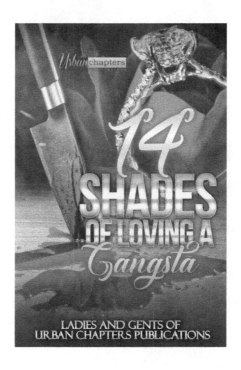